Healing Love

tions of this text, other than for review purposes, contact laurie@laurieryanauthor.com

QUALITY CONTROL: We strive to produce error-free books, but even with all the eyes that see the story during the production process, slips get by. So please, if you find a typo or any formatting issues, please let us know at laurie@laurieryanauthor.com so that we may correct it.

Thank you!

Acknowledgements

PUBLISHER'S NOTE: This is a sensual romance that blends heartfelt medical themes with holiday warmth and emotional discovery. Readers should be aware that the story includes:

References to cancer and cancer research

Medical settings, residency training, and patient care

Emotional themes of loss, grief, and vulnerability

Consensual sensual romance with open-door intimacy

At its heart, this novel celebrates healing, human connection, and the transformative power of love during life's most challenging moments.

From the author:

I hope you enjoyed Nicole's story. This contemporary romance grew out of a women's fiction story I wrote about her mother, Celia's valiant battle with ovarian cancer. You can read more about **Show Me** here.

At the point of reissuing this story, I've released fifteen novels and novellas to date. Each and every one of them has had a purpose, be it education, distraction, or my own healing.

Healing Love is no different as it's the final chapter of a family that helped me recover from the loss of a dear friend.

While I write some women's fiction and fantasy, my first love is romance and I like to add positive endings to contemporary issues, which can be found on my website.

DEDICATION

To medical personnel everywhere. From nurses to doctors, housekeeping to lab techs, I am grateful for you all.

CHAPTER ONE

Nicole Milbourne leaned in with a gloved hand to swab the patient's hive-covered leg for yet another culture. It shouldn't be this hard to diagnose a simple rash. Red blotches admittedly covered fifty percent of the patient's legs, so Nicole corrected her assessment. Maybe it wasn't so simple.

"Ouch."

The sound startled Nicole and the applicator flew out of her hand, settling with a soft thunk on the floor.

Nicole glanced at the portly woman she'd been assigned to follow up on. The head of the hospital bed was raised and the woman peered over her glasses at Nicole, her arms folded across her chest. With her lips set in a thin line of censure, it didn't take a body language expert to determine the woman's mindset.

"I'm sorry," Nicole said. "I didn't expect it would hurt."

"Well, it did," the woman answered. Her artificially carrot-colored hair didn't budge as she bobbed her head up and down.

Nicole tried to smile, certain it looked more like a jerky group of still frames end to end than a natural gesture of friendliness. If she couldn't carry on an ordinary conversation like this with a patient, how was she ever going to survive the residency program?

She reached for another swab kit.

"You're doing another culture?"

"Yes," Nicole said, focused on opening the stubborn paper and space-age plastic packet.

"Why?"

"It's possible we cultured too soon and the infection hadn't really taken hold, even though the symptoms were manifesting themselves."

The quiet whoosh of the hospital room door startled Nicole and the swab in her hand went spiraling to the floor. With a sigh, she reached for a third kit, quite certain it was going to be a very long three years.

Glancing up, her heart skipped about ten beats when her worst fears came true and the head resident walked in to the room.

Dr. Damien Reed was a legend in the halls of Rochester Regional. With an impressive scholastic resume', Kennedy looks, and a smile that could disarm the Middle East, the man was both respected by his peers and ogled by just about every woman in the place.

From a resident's perspective, that smile meant a thorough textbook grilling generally followed, which explained the pounding heart syndrome she got when she spotted him in the hallways.

Nicole had managed to escape his notice for her entire first week...almost. She clutched the swab kit. Today was day six of her residency.

She offered him a quick, professional nod and prayed he wouldn't ask her any questions. After taking a long moment scrutinizing her, he turned his charms on his patient. Nicole exhaled relief as she watched him interact with the woman.

"Mrs. O'Malley," he said with a wide grin as he held her hand between his and dug up some bad Irish charm. "And how are we doing this fine morning?"

As usual, Dr. Reed's dark hair was unkempt and shaggy. Nicole reached up to touch her own auburn hair, neatly captured in a bun at the nape of her neck, then remembered her gloved hands and dropped them to her side. The man's hair was reminiscent of a college student, not someone who'd risen to the position that put him in charge of newly indoctrinated medical residents. She tried to ignore jeans that fit too well, yet seemed completely inappropriate for someone with his status. This was Rochester Regional Medical Center, after all. There were protocols to be observed.

She studied him as he spoke with the patient and the conversation faded to gray. Even inappropriate, the hairstyle worked for him, framing a strong face, green eyes, and an effortless smile. No one appeared immune to his easy charm, least of all Mrs. O'Malley.

With the personality of a politician, everything seemed easy for Dr. Damien Reed. Not so for herself. A part of her envied him those skills.

Nicole yanked open another swab kit, surprised when it came apart in one pull and almost went flying again. When Dr. Reed's steady hands grasped hers as well as the kit, she chalked the slight quake in her arms up to first week nerves. If he held on longer than necessary, Nicole decided it had been to keep the swab from falling to the floor.

Nicole mumbled a thank you as Dr. Reed held out the swab for her to take.

"Anytime." Even the man's voice was designed for effect. The single word rolled off his tongue like warm honey. She could understand why patients sought him out. He made everything seem better with a simple word.

As Mrs. O'Malley ran down her list of complaints to Dr. Reed, Nicole, with extreme care this time, swabbed the rash, and then pulled the blanket back over the patient's leg.

"Thank you, dear. That was much better," Mrs. O'Malley said. "She was a bit rough on the first try," the patient explained to Dr. Reed, sending Nicole's already pink complexion into overdrive, if the warmth of her face was any indication. The man had the power to toss her out of the program with little or no reason, but he simply patted Mrs. O'Malley's hand and turned to Nicole.

For a moment, he held her gaze. When Nicole realized her lips were parted, she clamped them shut. Irritation replaced nerves when she watched his eyebrow lift in response.

"How are we on bringing this rash of Mrs. O'Malley's under control?"

Nicole took a deep breath. She would not be escaping his infamous grilling today, it appeared. Taking a moment, she reminded herself that this was where she excelled. She knew her diseases and what needed to be done to diagnose them. No one in the residency program would best her at diagnostic medicine. It was her strong point, as she'd proven over and over again in school.

Granted, Mrs. O'Malley's rash was being stubborn. The unexplained low grade fever was also an issue. But Nicole was certain she would determine the reason.

"We've done a blood work-up. Blood chemistry has all come back normal. As well, the first culture did not turn up a viable reason for the breakout. At this point, I've ruled out viral causes and am in the process of ruling out bacterial infections."

"It sounds like you've been very thorough, Doctor."

Nicole beamed. "Diagnosis has been elusive so far, but I feel confident we'll find the cause and get the patient back on track medically."

Mrs. O'Malley drank some of the water she'd picked up shortly after Dr. Reed entered the room.

"Thirsty?" he asked the patient.

She looked at the cup in her hand as if surprised. "It's strange. I never used to like water. Now I find myself sipping at it all day long."

Nicole frowned. What did that have to do with a rash?

Damien turned back to her. "Have you tested her blood sugar?"

Diabetes? He thought Mrs. O'Malley had *diabetes?* Nicole ran through the tests she'd ordered and the heat in her cheeks increased to inferno level. She wanted to crawl under the hospital bed and never come back out. No, she'd never tested the patient's blood sugar.

The medical encyclopedia in her head opened up to the page that dealt with complications of uncontrolled diabetes. Life threatening ones like coma and cellulitis were followed by lesser known symptoms. An unexplained rash was listed right there.

How could she have forgotten?

It took a real effort on her part to keep her hands from covering reddened cheeks. Oh, God, her first week here and she'd already screwed up. She shook her head. Well, there was nothing to do but own up to the colossal mistake she'd just made.

She glanced at her patient, who thankfully was busy watching Dr. Reed. "No, Doctor. I did not order a blood sugar. I'll be sure and order it stat."

"I think we'll have you fixed up in no time," he said to Mrs. O'Malley, patting her hand. What looked like a genuine smile on his face never wavered despite the fact he must be annoyed at the rookie mistake she'd just made. Even mortified as she was, she had to respect his ability to keep his emotions so well hidden.

"Can I speak to you outside, Dr. Milbourne?"

CHAPTER TWO

With her feet weighted by dread of the confrontation ahead of her, Nicole tried to hold her head high as she followed her boss out the door, certain she was about to be canned from the program.

Damien Reed put both hands in the pocket of his jeans and leaned back against the wall. The longer he stared across the corridor, the more Nicole began to sweat. This couldn't be good.

Well, better to confess up front than to wait and have it thrown in your face. "I'm sorry, Dr. Reed. I—I don't know why the possibility of a systemic disease like diabetes slipped my mind. I know better."

He closed his eyes. The look on his face was reminiscent of someone who'd just tasted heaven...or really great chocolate. When he opened them, she caught a quick flare of emotion before it disappeared behind his smile.

"Relax," he said. "Even if I thought you should be booted out of the program, I don't have the authority."

"Maybe not," she conceded. "But you have the ear of those who do."

He chuckled. "You've got me there." He pushed off the wall. "Walk with me."

She looked at the kit in her hand. "I really should get this to the lab."

Dr. Reed took it from her, pulled a pen from his pocket and, using the wall, wrote the patient's name and room number on it. Next, he waylaid a nurse. "Would you deliver this to the lab for me?"

"Certainly, Doctor." the nurse said. Twice his age, the woman glowed at the attention. Nicole rolled her eyes. The man had that affect on, well, just about everyone.

"Thank you," Nicole said to the nurse as she disappeared without any indication she'd heard Nicole's gratitude.

They walked in silence until he turned into a waiting room with nothing in it but a few chairs and neutral colors. Sitting, he motioned for her to take a chair across from him.

Here comes the boom. Nicole glanced at the picture above Dr. Reed's head. Did the sky over that sailboat indicate a storm was coming? Maybe. She settled her hands in her lap and waited.

"Why did you choose medicine for a career?"

The question came out of left field and Nicole felt her heart fill with the familiar ache of long ago memory. She clamped a lid on the pain and sat back, crossing her arms. "I don't see how that has any relevance to today."

"Humor me," he said. He leaned forward to rest elbows on knees, fingers laced together. "I'd like to understand your motivation."

"I have an interest in research," she finally answered. "Oncology research."

"That's on your resume. What I want to know is why?"

Nicole stared at green eyes that held both gentle question and firm resolve. She wasn't going to get out of answering. Over his head, the clouds in the picture seemed to darken. She didn't want to have this conversation, but he waited without moving until she finally answered.

"My mother passed away when I was ten years old."

"Cancer?"

She gave a quick nod. "Ovarian."

He cocked his head. "I'm sorry."

Nicole tried to shrug. She willed her shoulders to rise and show her indifference. Willed her head to remember that it had happened a long time ago. Willed her heart to stop thumping a painful reminder.

She should answer him. He was waiting, watching. After all these years, she still didn't know how to respond to that phrase. 'I'm sorry.' What the hell did that mean, anyhow? As she searched eyes filled with the patience of a man comfortable with silent pauses, she wanted, for the first time, to answer. "'I'm sorry' is such a strange phrase, don't you think? I'm not even sure I know what it means."

One dimple appeared. "It means something different for everyone. For me, it's all about what you went through, the pain you feel."

"Thank you." The unfamiliar sting of tears made her blink and her fingernails dug into her hands as she tried to regain some control. "I'm sure, Doctor, that you didn't call me in here for a therapy session."

He studied her for a long moment before making some sort of decision. "No. I didn't. But it is nice to know you're capable of showing some emotion."

She straightened. "I beg your pardon?"

He held up a hand. "Don't get your bristles standing at attention. I meant no insult."

"Is there some point to this discussion, Doctor Reed? Am I in trouble?"

"For missing a lab test during your first week here? No. That's what I'm here to help catch. What I would like to offer you is some advice."

Relief threatened what little control she had over her emotions. She wasn't getting fired? Some part of her brain recognized the word "advice" but she couldn't get past the echo in her ears. She still had a job.

"—see the patient."

He was speaking. The man who'd just given her future back to her was speaking. She needed to listen. "Excuse me?"

"I said," he repeated as he stood. "Take time to get to know the patient. Don't just look at the body, or the symptom. Talk to the patient. Much of the time, the answers can be found in a simple conversation."

She stood and scuffed the carpet with her shoe. "That's the hardest thing for me," she admitted.

He smiled again and Nicole found herself drawn to the warmth. "It will get easier. Trust me. In the meantime, remind yourself to ask questions and listen to what they say. It's generally the best place to start when trying to diagnose an issue."

"Thank you, Doctor."

"I don't stand on formalities with my team. Please, call me Damien."

She shook her head. "You're my superior. And you've earned the title of doctor."

"So have you, Nicole."

"I know the diploma says that, but I don't believe it. Not yet."

"Trust me, in this program, you'll have plenty of opportunities to recognize how much you've earned the title." He glanced at his watch. "I've got other residents to check on. But I'll be watching...your progress with interest."

After he left, Nicole sank back down in the chair. The emotional upheaval of the last few minutes had wiped her out. She felt like she'd just finished a twenty-four hour shift. According to the clock, she still had eight of her twelve hours to go and, when the patient load ran heavy like today, shifts ran long. She'd learned that her first couple days in the program. Certain it was going to be a very long day and an even longer residency, Nicole headed back to work.

With a blood glucose meter in hand, she returned to Mrs. O'Malley's room. Taking Dr. Reed's advice, she spent some time talking to her patient. Listened would be more accurate, since the woman seemed to enjoy an audience and, given the opening, warmed to any subject.

That conversation told her, even before she tested Mrs. O'Malley, that her patient was diabetic. All the symptoms were there, and had been for some time. Her high blood sugar only confirmed it. It also explained why the rash was not improving. Nicole wrote up orders for further testing to confirm the diagnosis on paper, as well as insulin to bring her blood sugars down and regular blood sugar monitoring. She explained the diagnosis to the patient and rose to leave.

When Mrs. O'Malley began to fret, Nicole's instinct to run came back full force. Panic felt like a noose around her neck. Comforting patients was not something they taught in med school. She patted her patient's arm, trying Dr. Reed's technique, but the movement felt jerky and trite.

Plus, it didn't help. Mrs. O'Malley had started to sniffle and Nicole felt the noose tighten. She struggled to shrug it off and considered their conversation. The woman lived alone. She had a son, but he lived an hour away.

"You know," she said. "You won't go through this alone."

"But I don't have anyone to help me," she said, dotting at her eyes with a tissue from the box Nicole handed her.

"You've got a hospital full of people to help. You'll be well regulated on insulin before you leave here. You'll be taught how to take care of yourself, both with your insulin and your diet."

The worried frown on Mrs. O'Malley's face didn't budge much. In fact, the lines in her forehead deepened a fraction.

"Diet? You mean, I have to change the way I eat?" She latched onto Nicole's hand. "Does that mean no more lunches with my Red Hat Society? You *do* know what that is, don't you, dear? It's a wonderful group of women and oh, they are so dear to me. Do I really have to refrain from lunches? Oh, how will I ever learn all this?"

"It's all right, Mrs. O'Malley," Nicole said as she tried to extricate her hand from the woman's grip. "You'll still be able to eat with your friends. You will have to be a bit careful about the menu choices you select, but diabetes is a very functional disease."

Instead of being reassured, Mrs. O'Malley's grip tightened until it bordered on painful. "Oh, my. That's right. Diabetes *is* a disease. I have a disease. Me, who's been healthy all her life. How will I ever explain this to my son? And to my friends?"

Nicole took a deep breath and dug deep for the words that would reassure her patient. "Diabetes is very common, Mrs. O'Malley. In fact, I wouldn't be surprised to find out a few of your society friends had diabetes."

The woman paused and loosened her grip enough for Nicole to free her hand.

"Do you think so?"

"I know so." Nicole tried not to smile as Mrs. O'Malley smoothed her blanket, the picture of calmness now.

"And—" Nicole said. "We will have Home Health nurses come and visit you after your discharge until you're comfortable with everything. As well, I'm sure your son will involve himself as much as he's able to."

That did the trick. The last lines on Mrs. O'Malley's face relaxed.

Then, to Nicole's horror, tears started to trickle down her patient's cheek. Lord, what had she said now?

"Thank you," Mrs. O'Malley said. "Thank you *so* much."

Nicole nodded, the lump in her throat a wall her voice couldn't break through. She backed toward the door.

"You know, dear," Mrs. O'Malley continued. "I think you're going to be a fine doctor."

On her way home that night Nicole pulled her collar tight against an unseasonable September chill and reflected on the lesson learned today. A few minutes of conversation had not only helped with diagnosis, it had also completely mollified an agitated patient.

Spending time in a one-on-one conversation hadn't been easy, though. A shyness that bordered on painful had plagued Nicole for years. That was a significant part of why research appealed to her. She'd been first in her class in both under-graduate and graduate schools, but she knew her people skills were lacking. She also knew that today she had learned a very important lesson about being a doctor. And that it would be the hardest personal limitation for her to overcome.

Dr. Reed had gone easy on her. She was certain of it, even though she didn't understand why. She smiled at the memory of her name spoken in the rich timber of his voice, then forced the thought to the back of her mind. It wouldn't do to start fantasizing over the hunky head resident. She had too much to accomplish before she could even think about any sort of relationship. She chuckled, knowing that it was silly to even consider the possibility. No way would the inimitable Dr. Reed be interested in her.

Inside her apartment, Nicole dropped her bag and coat over a threadbare, but comfy-enough-to-fall-asleep-studying-on couch and walked the few feet to her tiny kitchen.

Small by just about anyone's standards, Nicole's apartment was a haven to her. After promising the landlord she would return the walls to the non-descript ivory most rentals required, Nicole had painted the kitchen a pale tangerine color that made her smile each time she walked into the room.

She started water heating for tea she hoped would revive her enough to do some research tonight. As tired as she was, she wouldn't be able to sleep until she determined how she had missed that diagnosis of diabetes today.

She would not make that kind of mistake again. The unwavering green eyes of Damien Reed came to mind and she wondered whom she was working so hard to impress.

CHAPTER THREE

"Good morning, Ms. Grant. I'm Dr. Reed."

Nicole side-stepped into the emergency room alcove as Dr. Reed greeted the patient. He may have said that initial mistake of hers meant nothing, but his actions over the past two months told a different tale. It felt like he'd materialized around each and every corner she turned, always pinning her with questions and firing away with another one almost before she finished answering the last.

That he'd selected her as his pet project was pretty much a given. Because of that, life had bordered on a living hell, with twelve to twenty-hour shifts followed by several hours of studying. Tea had been relegated to the back of her kitchen cupboard as coffee became her new best friend.

Nicole wasn't sure how much more of his attention she could take. And if the man asked her one more time what the patient had to say, she was going to scream. He'd sent her back into hospital rooms to *talk* time and time again.

Yep. Dr. Reed had it out for her. She shook her head, knowing that wasn't entirely accurate. He'd offered some very insightful comments and suggestions during their debates. The man was a gifted diagnostician on top of being good with people.

At odd times, she'd turn and find him staring at her, his face a strange study of intensity. It was as if he had more to say, yet wouldn't. Or couldn't. Damien Reed was a mystery. One which, at the moment, she didn't have the time or the energy to figure out.

From her spot near the privacy curtain, Nicole observed the petite woman who was the focal point of her orientation to her E.R. rotation. With a smattering of freckles across the bridge of her nose and translucent skin, Nicole placed her age at close to her own twenty-eight years. She squinted. Very close, as a matter of fact. The woman looked familiar. Her hair color was similar to Nicole's, although the woman's ran a bit more to the red than her own darker curls.

"Amanda?"

Dr. Reed and the patient both turned to her.

"Nikki? Nikki Milbourne?"

Damien Reed's eyebrows raised up and Nicole's cheeks warmed with color. "I go by Nicole now."

"Wow," Amanda said. "What's it been? Ten years?"

"Easily," Nicole answered. Since Damien stood there with quiet expectancy, she turned to him. "Mandy and I were roommates our first year in college."

"Those were good times," Amanda said, smiling.

Nicole remembered. Loaded down with studies, she'd begged off almost all of Amanda's invitations to go out and have a little fun. Almost. She glanced at Dr. Reed and found him watching her with undisguised amusement. *Great.* All she needed was for him to think she was some sort of party animal.

"Good times and a lot of work," Nicole said in an attempt to dispel any wrong impressions. "You left, what? Mid-Winter quarter, right? I never heard from you after that."

"Yeah. Sorry about that. My Mom got sick, so I went home to take care of her."

"She must have been pretty sick."

"She was. Breast cancer."

"I'm sorry."

"Me, too. We caught it too late. After a couple years of surgeries and chemotherapy, the cancer won."

Nicole gripped Amanda's hand. "I know what that's like."

Amanda nodded, her voice turning wistful. "Anyhow, after all that, college didn't seem so important anymore. I was working already, so I never bothered to go back." She smiled, the sparkle returning to her eyes. "But all that time you spent with your head buried in books paid off. You're a doctor, huh? Good for you."

"Thank you. I'm doing my residency here at Rochester Regional." She glanced at Dr. Reed, who watched her with a bemused concentration she couldn't categorize. One thing she did know. It was past time to get back on track. "Our relationship means I can't be your physician," She told Amanda. She indicated Dr. Reed with her hand. "I'm confident Dr. Reed will take good care of you. And I'll stop by later to see how you're doing."

She turned to go, but Amanda held tight to her hand. "Please, stay." She worried her lower lip. "As my friend?"

Nicole hesitated, turning to Dr. Reed. He gave a quick nod of assent, so she moved around to the other side of the bed and stood silent as he began the process of diagnosing Amanda's pain. With his deep, mellow voice and quiet interest, he drew the information out.

Amanda Grant answered with confidence, even with the edge of worry Nicole could hear in her voice. She'd come to the emergency room with lower abdominal pain, primarily on the left side.

"How long have you had this pain, Ms. Grant?"

"Amanda will do just fine. Ms. Grant sounds like my career-minded maiden aunt." She smiled at Nicole. "No insult intended."

Nicole tucked her head as she stifled a grin.

"As for pain," Amanda said. "This time, it's been a day or so."

Nicole's head came up. "You've had this pain before?"

Dr. Reed glanced at her.

"Sorry to interrupt," she mumbled.

"A few times," Amanda answered. "It's been strange, kind of comes and goes." She grimaced. "Like now."

Dr. Reed continued. "On a scale of one to ten, how would you rate your pain at the moment?"

"About a five or six." The grunt as she finished the sentence validated her pain level. It took a few moments before she could continue. "It's been getting harder to ignore these last couple of months. I know I should have gone to my doctor, but work has been so crazy." She frowned and her hands settled across her abdomen. "This time, it's stronger than ever." She glanced at Nicole. "And it doesn't seem to be going away."

"What does the pain feel like?"

"It's like a deep ache. And low, off to the left."

Nicole felt a trickle of sweat begin to work its way down her spine as she fought to stay objective. Amanda's pain seemed localized, but it could still be one of many issues. It could be an inflammation in the colon, or kidney stones, or any number of things.

Or it could be ovarian pain. The thought sliced through her like a scalpel.

"Have you noticed any other issues?"

"Well, I've been more tired lately. That could be because I'm not eating all that well. Food just hasn't tasted that good."

Mental fingers in Nicole's brain went back to ticking off the illnesses that could account for these symptoms.

"I feel like I'm bloated. Then, yesterday I started to wonder if I had a bladder infection."

Hands curling into tight fists, Nicole fought for every ounce of strength she had to keep from backing up as dread tightened around her spinal column. She knew these symptoms. She turned wide eyes to Dr. Reed. At the imperceptible shake of his head, she forced her fingers to straighten and her hands to relax. She tried to focus on what Damien was saying but worry filled her ears with cotton.

Once he'd completed the physical examination and found tenderness in more than one spot, he turned to Nicole.

"What tests would you order, Doctor?"

Amanda grinned. "He's quizzing you, right?"

Nicole started to answer, but felt like she was chewing sand. Taking a moment to clear her throat, she recited a litany of tests she'd studied well over the course of her post-graduate studies.

"I'd order standard blood tests to check for an infection, as well as a—" Her voice broke and Amanda Grant's dimple disappeared.

"Sorry," Nicole muttered as another bead of sweat wound its way down her back. "Frog in my throat. I'd also order a…a CA-125, and a trans-vaginal ultrasound."

Dr. Reed nodded. "I concur." He turned to the patient. "We probably can't get some of these tests until tomorrow. I suggest we keep you in the hospital overnight."

"Oh, but I've got a meeting tomorrow that I have to be at."

Cancel it! Nicole wanted to scream the words, but she kept her lips tightly compressed.

"Can you bump it?" The casual warmth of Dr. Reed's tone was in direct opposition to the bile rising in Nicole's throat.

"Keeping you here means we'll get results faster," he said. "As well, we can do more to alleviate your pain in a hospital setting. Your pain was enough to bring you here, so it might be a good idea to give us some time to get it under control for you."

Back to worrying her lip, Amanda nodded her agreement.

Once out of the room, Nicole felt tears well up that were beyond her control. She started to shake. *Is it getting hot in here?* She tugged at the neckline of her shirt.

"I…need…some…air," she gasped.

Dr. Reed took her by the elbow and steered her out the emergency room doors, grabbing a blanket off the supply rack as he went by. Outside, he didn't stop until Nicole smelled the stale lingering scent of cigarettes. They were in the smoking shack? Thankfully, it was empty at the moment.

Nicole plopped into a chair. She knew Amanda Grant's symptoms and in fact, had studied them in depth. She gulped air in and felt a hand urge her head down between her legs as a blanket settled around her.

"Breathe, Nicole." His low tone soothed her, but not enough. She struggled to sit up.

Damien Reed wouldn't let her. Instead his hand moved across her back. The up and down motion, along with the sound of his voice saying words she'd didn't understand, eventually calmed her.

After several long moments, he allowed her up and snugged the blanket tighter around her shoulders. "Feeling better?"

"No." She shook her head. Curls that had escaped her bun settle around her face. "I mean yes, but no." She reached for his arm. "I know those symptoms. I *know* them because of my mother."

"It's too soon to know for sure."

"Everything adds up. All her symptoms point to an ovarian problem."

"Even if they do, it could be as simple as cystic ovaries. As a physician, you know better than to draw a conclusion before testing."

Nicole shot out of the chair and glared at him, the blanket falling to the cement. "Yes, I do. Except that I've studied this disease in depth. I know—"

His hand rose and, for a moment, Nicole thought he intended to touch her cheek. Then he dropped it to his side. "Don't make assumptions, Nicole. Wait for confirmation."

"I can't." The words came out on the end of a sob as she whirled on him. "Did you know what was wrong before you drew me in there?" She choked on the words. "Did you set me up for some sort of shock therapy?"

"I knew no more than you did. I think you know I wouldn't do that to you."

"It doesn't look good, does it?" Nicole whispered the words, afraid saying them out loud would make it real.

Damien picked up the blanket and settled it once again around her shoulders. "We won't know for sure until the tests come back."

He sank to a chair and massaged his temples. He was as affected by this as she was. She knew it, but overriding that realization was an almost paralyzing return to the day her mother had explained her own cancer.

Memories Nicole had struggled to bury for years resurfaced. She sat back down, tucking her hands underneath her. Too keyed up to remain that way, she hugged herself. Her breath frosted in the late November air and the ground sparkled with cold crystals. She didn't feel the chill. She was too overwhelmed by memories.

Damien's voice filtered through. "This isn't your mother, Nicole. It sounds tough, but you're going to see this situation a lot."

"I know that," she said. The words sounded hollow and far away.

His hand reached over to move a strand of hair out of her eyes. He stared at her hair as it curled around his fingers for a long moment before he pulled away. "This will sound harsh, but you need to decide if you can handle it."

Nicole jumped up and started to pace. "No." She shook her head, and then reached to pin her hair back into its usual bun. "I don't have to handle it. Or get used to it. I refuse to. This shouldn't have to happen. Not to her, not to my mother, not to anyone." She pounded her fists against her thighs. "*That's* why I've selected oncology research. So that the Amanda Grants of the world don't have to hear what you're most likely going to have to tell her in a couple days."

Damn it. She was so angry her body shook. And now she could feel the spilled tears on her face. Dr. Reed joined her. He tipped her head up and one thumb brushed at a wayward tear.

Nicole stared into eyes that showed compassion...and something else. She watched little lines deepen at the corners of those eyes as he smiled.

"I believe you will do just that, Nikki."

Damien Reed surprised the hell out of her then as he pulled her into his arms. Only for a brief moment, then he released her and turned away, his deep intake of breath surprising her.

Nicole felt bereft. She wanted to stay in those warm, comforting arms. To be soothed by them. By him.

"Dr. Reed?" A nurse rounded the corner.

He stepped in front of Nicole, giving her time to get her tears under control.

"Yes?"

"We'll need orders to admit the patient in room six. And we've got victims en route from a multi-car accident. Dr. Jones asked if you could stay and help with triage."

Most people would miss the slump to his shoulders. Nicole noticed it, as well as the quick recovery. He wasn't untouched by the plight of the patients he treated. She wiped the last remaining dampness from her face. How much time would it take to develop a professional shell like his? *Too long*. She'd be well ensconced in a research facility long before she could grow the same hardened facade.

"Tell Dr. Jones I'll be right there," Dr. Reed said.

Once the nurse was gone, he turned back to Nicole. "I know patients like this are going to affect you."

"They affect you, too, don't they?"

He nodded. "They do. But I've had a little more time to figure out how to process it all."

"I can't imagine it ever being easy."

"Not easy, just easier to compartmentalize. You'll need to find a way to steel yourself no matter what the patient's issue is."

She sighed, knowing he was right.

He settled a hand on her shoulder. "I'll help you," he said. He took a few steps toward the E.R. doors and then turned back. "Get yourself together and join me for triage." His voice deepened. "And please, call me Damien."

She shook her head.

"I insist," he said with a grin as he disappeared.

Unable to get Amanda Grant off her mind, Nicole stopped in later that day. She found Amanda chewing away on her lower lip. "What's up?"

"Either this hospital works fast or you've got some pull around here, Doctor. The nurse just told me I'm going for that ultrasound test you ordered. They'll be here any minute."

Nicole chuckled. "Hospital time runs about the same as football time. It could be an hour or more." Hearing a commotion behind her, Nicole rolled her eyes. "They're here now, aren't they? Proving me wrong?"

Amanda leaned onto one elbow to see who or what was behind Nicole. With eyes no longer showing any trepidation, she nodded, a wide grin on her face.

A sense of satisfaction turned a bad day good for Nicole. She'd made Amanda forget, at least for a moment. On impulse, she offered to go with her to the test and Amanda's acceptance was quiet but heartfelt. When the procedure got a little uncomfortable and Amanda reached for her hand, Nicole tried to steel herself from the emotional double whammy. She cared about Amanda Grant. Add to that the realization that her mother had endured this same testing, and Nicole failed to find any sort of guard rail for her heart. Empathy wrapped its arms tightly around her and she couldn't honestly tell who was holding on tighter, she or Amanda.

CHAPTER FOUR

At home that evening, Nicole took the salad she'd thrown together over to the table and sat down. It had been a long day and she was, once again, bone tired. With a sigh she looked at the pile of case histories she needed to review.

She picked at her lettuce, but wasn't hungry. Amanda Grant's situation overshadowed everything. Nicole was not well-versed in ultrasound images. At the moment, she was grateful for that lack of knowledge. She didn't want Amanda to see her recognize the worst case scenario. Hell, she didn't want Amanda to hear that scenario from her or anyone else.

She'd re-read the same paragraph three times when her phone rang.

"Hi, Nikki."

"Dad!" Her father must be psychic. How else did he manage to call every time she needed a shoulder? "I'm glad you called." She tried to keep the quaver out of her voice.

"I thought I'd call and see how my best girl is doing. What's up?"

"Nothing. Everything's fine," she said.

"It doesn't sound like it. This is Dad you're talking to. Come on. Fess up."

He could always see through her attempts at being tough. "It's just been a long day."

"Long how?"

She sighed. He wasn't going to let her off the hook. She knew that. "I started my E.R. rotation today."

"You were looking forward to that, weren't you?"

"I was."

"Hmmmm. And now something has you not so enthused?"

"I had a tough patient to start out with."

"Tough how?"

Between hospital privacy laws and her knowledge that mentioning her mother would bother him, Nicole was unsure what to say.

"I let a patient get to me," she answered.

"Get to you? Get to you how? Did someone attack you, Nicole? Are you all right? Do I need to come out there?"

She laughed. Leave it to her father to misinterpret. The man's tendency to leap without thought was legendary. He'd explained one time how this issue, not an absence of love, had caused the demise of his marriage to her mother. "She wanted a security I wasn't able to give her," he'd said.

Nicole knew her step-mother had managed to settle him down, and just in time, too, since her mother's death had led to a whirlwind courtship and wedding. Kate had taken over raising her and had done a good job. As good as she could.

Never able to have children herself, Kate had immersed their household in a revolving door of foster children. So much so that Nicole had always felt a bit like an outcast in her own home. She wasn't chosen. She'd come with her father as part of the package.

"Nicole? Are you all right?"

"Yes, Dad. Stop worrying. I didn't get attacked."

"Then what…" His voice, tinny through the phone, still made Nicole feel he was here in the room with her.

"I had a patient with some familiar, um, symptoms."

She could almost hear her father digesting the statement, searching for the positive spin. And then, unable to find it, coming to the right conclusion.

"Symptoms like what happened with your mother?"

"Yes." She whispered the word, wondering if she should knock on wood so as to not jinx Amanda Grant. She felt, deep inside, that no amount of woodwork could help her friend.

"And that hit you smack in the heart, didn't it?"

She pulled her feet up onto the kitchen chair, hugging her knees close enough to lay her cheek on, certain she could hear her heart pounding. "Yes."

She waited. Her father could always find the optimist's point of view. He could cheer her up when no one else could and he'd come through now, she was certain of it. He'd always come through in those clutch times. Which was why his next statement caught her so off guard.

"Honey, I know losing your Mom was tough. If this is too hard for you, maybe you should give it up. Come home and find a different line of work."

She jumped to her feet. "No. Absolutely not. I *want* to be a doctor. I have to. I *have to* find a cure."

"How are you going to get through this residency program? You're already mired in the same emotional empathy I saw in you as such a young child when your mother was sick." He sighed. "I know you. I know how hard you've guarded your heart since then. Almost to the point where you don't show emotions, period. If this patient is bringing all those feelings to the surface, what will the next patient do? I hate to say it, but this is going to happen again and again and again. You know that."

"Yes, I do know. It's funny that you say I guard my emotions. Damien says I need to toughen my skin. That it doesn't get easier, but it gets easier to deal with emotionally."

"Who's Damien?"

"Oh, sorry. I meant to say Dr. Reed."

"Isn't he that lead resident you've been complaining about since you started this program? How he's been picking on you and making you work harder than anyone else?"

"Yes. That's him."

"I see," her father said. "So, when did you get on a first name basis with someone who, up to this point, has seemed more like your nemesis?"

Nicole's mouth dropped open as she realized her mistake. "He's, umm, still driving me hard." She tried to keep her tone neutral, in complete opposition to her flaming cheeks.

The laughter on the other end of the line indicated she hadn't pulled it off. *Damn.* "I didn't mean to call him Damien. And I don't. Not at work."

"You see him outside of work?"

"Never! He just...he asked me to call him Damien, all right?"

"Oh, really." He drew the word out in a way that teetered on very dangerous, very match-makerlike, territory. "This is starting to sound serious."

Nicole's mind churned as she tried to find a way out of this conversation. Her father, a man to whom everything was funny, would not let this go. She gave it one last futile attempt.

"It's not like that. It's nothing but a working relationship. Even that will only last a few months. He's finishing up his final year of residency. That's why he's the lead."

"So he'll only be your boss a few more months, huh?"

Nicole could hear the laughter in his voice. "Drop it, Dad. I'm telling you, it's not like that. Not. At. All." Nicole suppressed the twinge of pain her words caused. Dr. Reed was the head of her team and nothing more. Really.

Then why do I keep remembering how good it felt to be in his arms?

"You know how much your mother and I would like you to find someone to share your life with," her father said.

Lord, could this conversation get any worse? "I know. But not right now. I need to focus on getting through this residency and settled into my research. There's plenty of time to meet someone after that. So, how's Kate doing?"

This time, he let her off the hook. "Oh, fine."

"Your tone doesn't sound fine to me."

"She's a little lost right now. No kids in the house, you know?"

Nicole chuckled. "Kate's always been happiest when she's chasing after children."

"Yes, she has. You know, she's your mother, too. It would be nice if you called her by that title."

Nicole straightened. They'd had this conversation before. "Has she said something?"

"No. And she never will," her father said.

Nicole felt the weight of her father's request once again settle on her shoulders. Her mother had died when she was ten years old. No one could replace her. "I'm sorry. I just...can't."

Her father was so quiet that she said his name again to make sure he was still there.

"I'm here. And I understand, even if I'm disappointed. *Kate* is actually the reason for my call. I think we need a change of pace."

Nicole frowned and looked outside her window. Even in the dark she could see light flakes signaling the season's first snow fall. "What kind of change?"

"Well, Kate's been sort of at loose ends. With no children in the house, and you on the other side of the country, I considered this might be a good opportunity for us to take a vacation. You know, get away from Seattle for a bit?"

Nicole sat up. "You're coming to visit? That would be great!" She looked around her tiny apartment and wondered how she'd fit them in, and then realized it didn't matter. They'd find room.

"Actually, I was thinking more along the lines of finding some warmer weather. I've booked us on a Caribbean cruise."

Somewhat deflated, Nicole got up and tossed her salad in the trash. "A cruise sounds like fun."

"I think it will be. I'm telling her about it tonight."

"I'm sure she'll love it."

"Here's the thing, Babydoll. We leave on Christmas Eve."

"Christmas Eve?" Her mind whirled. "But...I always come home for Christmas."

"I know. And I know how important that is to you. I think you know it's important to us, too."

Nicole's eyes stung with the effort to hold her emotions in check. Her chest felt like the weight of the world had just landed on top of it. Christmas was the one thing in her life that had never changed. Her mother had loved it. Her father and Kate had recognized that and made a big deal of the holiday.

"Here's the thing. Kate hasn't just been at loose ends. I'm worried she's depressed. She just sits all day and waits for the phone to ring...for another child to put her arms around. I think a change of pace might break her out of that melancholy."

She could very well believe that Kate was struggling. She knew what the kids meant to her. But to cancel Christmas? "I-I guess I understand."

"I knew you would. Thanks, honey. I know if I can get her to take the first step, she'll love the vacation."

Leaning against the counter, Nicole took a deep breath. "I'm sure she will. And I know the trip will be good for both of you."

"I think so, too. Now all I have to do is convince your mother."

"Good luck with that. I don't remember the last time you two went anywhere alone together."

"It's been a few years."

"Well, let me know how it goes when you tell her, okay?"

"I will. Thanks. I know this won't be the Christmas you're used to. But, you know, change can also mean opportunity. Maybe something will come up that will be even better than spending the holidays with us."

Nicole shook her head so hard curls hit her in the cheek. "Nothing beats Christmas at home."

"We'll see. In the meantime, you won't get away from us completely. We'll try to find a way to call you on Christmas Day. And I'm sure Kate will be mailing you a package."

Nicole hung up the phone, and then sat back down at the table. After several minutes of staring at blurry words, she gave up and headed for the couch and some mindless reality show on television.

Christmas. Her favorite day of the entire year. Her mother had loved the season and decorated their house from top to bottom each year, even when she'd been so sick with cancer she could barely stand. She'd also always made sure Nicole's father shared in the celebration, something very few divorced couples could work out.

After...after her mother passed away, Kate had worked hard to make sure Christmas continued to be a special day for Nicole and for all of them.

Nicole had already spent Thanksgiving in the hospital cafeteria. With this change to Christmas, her entire holiday season was in an upheaval. This would be a first for her, not spending the holidays at home. And Nicole couldn't quite get past the worry that Christmas, for her, was forever changed.

CHAPTER FIVE

Nicole wandered through hospital halls she probably knew better than her own apartment. She'd lost interest in the cheerful holiday decorations that adorned dull white walls and gleaming countertops, surrendering to the blurred dullness of too many long shifts. Another one of which she had just finished.

If she could make it to the intern's lounge without any more emergencies cropping up, Nicole could claim a few precious hours of sleep. She'd need them to get through her next twenty-hour rotation. Going home to her apartment was not an option due to time constraints and the December snowstorm that had dumped a foot of snow in the Rochester area.

Bone-tired now had meaning for her. It was all she could do to focus on putting one foot in front of the other.

"Ooomph!"

The stillness of night shift was broken by her collision with Brenda, one of the nurses.

"Sorry," Nicole said.

Nicole had shared some late night conversations with the nurse during rare quiet times. Primed for pre-med, Brenda had happily let pregnancy derail her. Nurturing was in her blood and the woman was good at it. Brenda eyed her now like a parent checking her child for injuries. "Are you all right?"

"Yes," Nicole said, hearing the weariness in her voice. "Just tired."

"Forgive me for saying this, but you look a little like death warmed over. You need some sleep, Doctor."

Nicole's head came up. Even after three months as a resident, she still wasn't used to the title of doctor. "I'm headed for sleep now." She glanced at her watch. Only five hours to her next rotation. "I hope I get enough to get through tomorrow. After that, I get an entire fourteen hours off." A weak smile was the only enthusiasm she could muster.

Brenda's smile showed her sympathy. "Get some sleep while you can," she said. She started to walk away, but turned back. "Hey, have you seen Dr. Reed?"

"Uh, not recently." *Thank goodness.* How could just the idea of Damien Reed make her feel so hyper-sensitive? It was like her skin remembered his touch. Nicole rubbed her arms as she asked Brenda why she needed Dr. Reed.

"His migraine patient is pretty miserable. I wondered if we could increase her pain meds."

Trying to shake the fuzz from her brain, Nicole asked Brenda if there was anything she could do to help the patient.

"No, no. I'll page Dr. Reed. You," she said, wagging a finger at Nicole, "get some sleep while you can."

Nicole tossed a grateful wave in the air and dragged herself down the hall to the break room, praying it would be empty. No more conversations. She needed sleep.

The lights were low in the lounge, but she could see empty couches and she offered a quick prayer of thanks. Grabbing a pillow and blanket off the pile pilfered from various linen carts, she took a grateful step toward one of the couches.

The scrape of a chair turned her in the opposite direction, where the illumination from a small desk lamp verified she wasn't, in fact, alone.

Dr. Damien Reed sat hunched over a book. Nicole craned her neck to see what he was reading. It looked like a medical manual. He didn't even twitch an ear at her arrival which was unusual.

Over the past few weeks, he'd been everywhere. Each time she turned a corner, ordered a lab test, or evaluated a new patient, he was either involved or nearby. That presence should have calmed her. Instead, she found it difficult to focus. She learned firsthand that his reputation for patient advocacy was fairly earned. Even more than that, he cared about his patients.

She respected him for that. And told herself for the hundredth time that is was his professionalism she was drawn to.

His shaggy hair was more unkempt than usual. It stood out at angles in strange spots, as if he'd been running his hands through it and stopped midway. He'd taken his lab coat off. It sat crumpled on the chair next to the desk.

Muscles rippled across his back as he turned a page. How did the man stay in such good shape when he spent almost every waking minute here at the hospital? She barely remembered to eat, let alone exercise.

Damien hung his head. The sigh he emitted echoed through the room, sending vibrations of compassion through Nicole. She glanced longingly at the bedding she held, and then tossed it aside and poured two cups of coffee.

Nicole tried to set the cup on the desk with care. She really tried. What she hadn't factored in was his complete focus on the textbook in front of him. The cup hit the desk for all of two seconds and then went airborne in response to his reflexive startle. The coffee stain spread down her lab coat in mocha-colored fingers. Nicole stared down at it, then up into the shocked face of Damien Reed.

"I'm sorry," he said.

She pulled the soggy jacket off, wadded it up, and tossed it into a nearby laundry bin. "Lab coats are a dime a dozen. It's my fault. I shouldn't have surprised you."

His only response was a quick nod as he turned back to the textbook.

"What? No retort?"

Damien didn't answer and that's when Nicole started to worry. She pulled his lab coat from the chair and sat down. As she settled the jacket on her lap, she smelled something all male. It wasn't cologne. They weren't allowed to wear it due to allergy issues. It was Damien Reed's scent, warm spice with a touch of hospital antiseptic thrown in, and it drew her in. Nicole clenched her jaw against the desire to bury her face in the coat.

When she looked up, she could see his eyes almost as unfocused as hers and as red as a student in a No-Doze cram session for finals. She knew the look and most likely mirrored it, except with him, deep worry lines around his eyes and mouth enhanced the weariness.

"Are you all right?"

He scrubbed his face with his hands. "I'm fine. It's my patient I'm worried about."

Nicole knew about worry. This residency seemed to have broken through that self-imposed emotion-guard her father had mentioned. She'd worried and fretted over too many patients these past few months and she wasn't sure she could handle the repetitive ache of concern.

In an attempt to lighten Damien's mood, she asked him what happened to compartmentalizing work.

His answering scowl proved how truly concerned he was.

"What's up?"

"I try not to worry. Most of the time, it works. This one's tough. I hate to see people in pain."

"End-stage situation?"

"I don't know." He rubbed his chin. "God, I hope not."

Nicole reached out to comfort him, but pulled back unsure of how that would be received. She wanted to smooth the lines from his forehead and see again the smile she'd become accustomed to. Instead, she clutched his lab coat in her hands. Sentiment, however well-meaning, would not help him solve his patient's dilemma.

Leaning an arm on the desk, she quizzed him. "What symptoms does the patient present with?"

The ghost of that smile she wanted to see returned as he straightened. "So the lead resident now becomes the student?" he asked.

She arched an eyebrow in response and it took only a moment before he grabbed the bait.

"All right, Doctor. A twenty-two year old female arrived about twelve hours ago with debilitating head pain, photosensitivity, and extreme emotional distress."

"Did you *talk* to the patient?"

This time, he did break out in a smile. "In depth."

"Social history?"

"Mother and father are still alive. Two siblings. No family history I can relate to this."

Nicole nodded. "Has she had anything like this before?"

"No."

"What's going on in her life right now?"

"The family's not well off. She entered college early and has been funded almost completely by scholarships and grants. She also finished early and is cramming for her GRE exam for graduate school."

"Could this be stress related?"

"Possibly." He cocked his head. "We can't rule that out."

"Migraine?"

"It appears so, except the standard medication regimen isn't doing much to alleviate her pain."

"Have you done a spinal tap?"

Damien nodded. "Yes. In fact, I was pinning my hopes on meningitis being the issue, but the test was negative."

Nicole was at a loss. "That about takes care of any possibilities I can think of without doing more research."

The buzz of Damien's pager sounded harsh in the quiet room.

"That about your patient?"

"Yes." Damien pushed off the desk and stood.

Nicole stood with him, handing him the now wrinkled lab coat. "Maybe talking to her again would give you more clues?"

"I agree," he said. "But I need to get her pain under control first."

"Would you like me to go with you?"

One side of his mouth quirked up. He reached to brush a strand of hair back from her face and traced a tender line down her cheek. "No. However I look, you look worse."

"Thanks," she said with a laugh that vanished under the intensity of his gaze. Tough patients, sleep deprivation, everything negative in her life at the moment faded as she let her eyes show what her words could not. She cared for Damien Reed much more than she should.

She no longer felt tired. In fact, she wanted this moment to go on forever. His hand cupped her chin. Her eyes dipped to his lips. She'd let his smile lull her to sleep more nights that she could recall. Now, desire overrode sense. She wanted to feel those lips on hers.

He lowered his head one agonizing centimeter at a time. Nicole's breath was nothing but infinitesimal puffs of air as she waited for the touch she'd dreamed about.

The door behind them creaked open and another resident stepped in. "Oh," he said. "Sorry."

Nicole never did figure out how Damien managed to put distance between them so fast. "No need to be sorry," he told the doctor. He stared at Nicole for a long moment before motioning to the couch. "Get some shut-eye." Without another word, he strode out of the room.

Nicole stared at the door long after it closed behind Damien. Her hand went to the lips he had almost touched. *What had just happened?* Always gentle, he was hands-on with his patients, but maintained a hands-off policy with the residents. The frustrated rumor-mill was proof of that.

When she noticed the resident watching her, she grabbed the bedding from the floor and headed for a couch. Damien could have any woman in the hospital if he wanted. On more occasions than she could count, she'd overhead invitations. For dinner, for drinks, even suggestions of more intimate gatherings. Nicole frowned.

Why would he almost kiss her? And, why, oh why hadn't he been faster at it.

She scowled at the interrupting resident, and then settled back into the pillow to let dreams of a dark-haired physician carry her off to sleep.

The jarring pager vibration, her wakeup call, brought Nicole around to a groggy reality. She blinked her eyes several times, trying to dispel the fog that saturated her vision. She recognized the break room and sat up, rubbing her eyes to help them stay open.

It didn't work. A glance at her watch explained why. She'd gotten a mere three hours of sleep. Nicole leaned against the couch back, running fingers through her hair and wondering how she was ever going to survive in this sleep-deprived state.

Standing to stretch still tired muscles, Nicole sniffed. The odor of burnt coffee permeated the air. *Great.* Someone left an empty pot on a hot burner...again.

After cleaning the pot and starting a new one, she went down the hall to freshen up. Glancing in the mirror, she was dismayed at the circles under her eyes. Not black, but certainly an early charcoal. She pulled at the skin on her cheek. Was it losing its elasticity? When was the last time she'd been outside or seen sunshine?

With coffee in hand, Nicole decided to check on Dr. Reed's patient before starting her own shift. She stepped into the darkened room and found him slumped over in a chair on the far side of the hospital bed, asleep.

"He's been like that for an hour or so now."

The whisper came from the bed and Nicole turned to the patient. She wasn't much younger than Nicole, but frailty stole years. She appeared petite, and maybe a little underweight. Her brown hair hung limp. Her eyes were open, and even in the darkness, Nicole could tell they were a startling lavender color.

Nicole smiled. Her voice barely above a whisper, she cocked her head toward the man in the chair. "So I caught the boss sleeping on the job, eh?"

The girl let out a soft chuckle, but even that effort creased her brow.

Nicole held out her hand. "I'm Dr. Milbourne, one of the residents here."

"Mary Smith," she said, giving Nicole's hand a feeble shake.

"Pain still bad?"

"It's...a little better."

"But not much," Nicole said.

"No." She tried to shake her head, but the grimace on her face said even that was too much movement.

"Don't try to move. I just stopped by to see if I could help." She motioned to the chair. "I see you're in good hands."

"I...just wish this pain would go away." Tears welled up in the lilac eyes.

"If anyone can find out what the problem is, it's Dr. Reed," Nicole said. It wasn't much, but she felt the need to offer the girl hope.

"Thank you for that vote of confidence, Dr. Milbourne."

Nicole's head shot up as Damien Reed straightened. He had a clearly defined five o'clock shadow. Nicole had never been attracted to beards, but on him, it looked good. Too good. The vision of that cheek up against hers warmed her own face to the point where she was glad the lights were low.

Keeping her voice quiet, she asked if there was anything she could do to help.

"Not unless you've got a suggestion for pain reduction," he said as he rubbed sleep out of his face.

"I'd be up for that," Mary said.

Nicole smiled at the patient. "I've seen how hard Dr. Reed's working to reduce your pain level."

"I know he is. And it's worked—a little," she said.

"But not enough," Damien finished, his lips thin lines. "I've ordered a CT scan."

Nicole nodded, knowing a scan would be to rule out bleeding issues. Checking her watch, she realized she was just about overdue for rounds. "I've got to go, but if there's anything I can do to help, page me."

"Thank you," Damien said. His eyes mirrored the gratitude in his voice and Nicole carried that memory with her through another long day of patient care.

CHAPTER SIX

Nicole set her tray on a cafeteria table and slumped down into a chair. It was way too late to be eating dinner, but she needed something in her stomach. She took a bite of mashed potato, grimaced, and set her fork down. How could her stomach growl even as her throat closed up, unwilling to swallow?

It had been the day from hell. She'd picked the worst day to be late for rounds. Dr. Jones, the attending physician who oversaw the entire residency program had chosen today to pop in and supervise the residents. She'd heard he did this to the first-year students as a way to catch them off guard and wean the ones who couldn't take the pressure.

Not a good day to show up late. He'd noted her entrance with nothing more than a glance. He then proceeded to chose her for the worst and most menial tasks for the remainder of the day. Nicole had worn a path in the linoleum going back and forth to the lab. He'd asked her for initial impressions with each new case. At least she'd held her own in that respect. So far, she was five for five on her diagnoses being correct.

Then she'd gone in to treat little Riley Macon. Nicole palmed her forehead in frustration. A simple fracture, Dr. Jones had said. But Nicole had observed much more while casting the boy. Eight years old, he appeared more like a six year old. His hunched stature, like the mother who would not let go of his hand, didn't feel right. The father stood in the corner with his arms crossed and no one said a word except to answer a question. Their answers were monotoned and monosyllabic.

"Yes, Doctor."

"No, Doctor."

That was all she could get out of them. When she'd tried to help the boy take his shirt off, he'd clutched it to his body. Not, however, before she'd caught a glimpse of a dark bruise. Knowing something wasn't right, she'd muttered something about needing additional supplies and searched out the attending, who, with multiple victims en route from an accident, had been very clear about his lack of interest in her concerns.

"Discharge him now, Dr. Milbourne. Let his primary care physician handle it. We need the room for more serious cases."

Instead, Nicole had pulled up hospital records showing three visits in the last six months, all for unrelated injuries. Then she'd called social services, who called child protective services.

The father had been removed from the room against his will. It had taken several guards to subdue him and he was now in police custody. Nicole stood in the back of the room as the mother and boy revealed, word by slow word, a long history of mental and physical abuse.

They'd get the help they needed now.

Deepened lines on Dr. Jones' face illustrated his annoyance with her as he overheard her being congratulated for seeing the true issue. She'd pay for going over his head. That much was certain.

"Rough day?"

Nicole looked up to see Damien standing there with a tray. She waved to the other seat at her table and he joined her.

"Let's see." She started ticking off reasons on her fingers. "I was late for rounds, so your boss used me as his personal sounding board and errand girl. Then I went against his orders on a case, so I'm guessing my life is going to change from an exhausted purgatory to a living hell for a while."

He chuckled. "I heard what you did for that boy and his mother."

How could he have heard?

"It may be a large hospital, but the really juicy stories get around quick. And shaming the man most nurses love to hate is definitely news that moves." He chewed a bite of his sandwich before speaking again. "You did the right thing, you know."

Nicole nodded. She knew. Hearing him say it made her feel better. She picked up her fork and started in on her salad.

They ate in companionable silence until her cell phone rang. Damien made a move to leave, but Nicole waved him to stay. "It's my Dad. I'm sure it won't take long."

"Hi, Nikki," Kate said.

So it wasn't her Dad. "Hi, Kate. How's everything going?"

"As well as can be expected. Honey, your father told me about the cruise he booked."

The trip that had changed everything about Nicole's holiday. She tried to stifle the resentment, but it wasn't easy. "You should have fun," she said.

"I told him I couldn't agree without talking to you, dear. I know how much the holidays mean to you. We won't go on this cruise without your blessing."

Nicole felt the power shift to her. She felt Kate's honest need for her consent. And she felt like a heel for her role in Kate's needing that approval.

It appeared she would be spending her first Christmas alone. She glanced at Damien, but he appeared more interested in finding a way through the saran wrap that encased a chocolate chip cookie than in her conversation.

She closed her eyes. *Buck up, Nicole. It's only one holiday.* She tried. She tried really hard, but the quaver in her voice didn't quite disappear. "Go. Have fun. You've more than earned this." She smiled, hoping the action would infuse her voice with cheerfulness. "Fun is good for the spirit, you know. I'm a doctor. I should know."

"But you'll be alone for Christmas," Kate said.

Ouch. The stark realization hurt, but she again snuffed the seed of resentment as much as she could. "It's only one holiday, right? We've had a lot of them and we'll have a lot more. I'm thrilled for both of you, getting away for this first time ever on a vacation by yourselves. Honest."

"Thank you, dear. I know this must not be easy for you. You know we'll miss you, don't you?"

She tried not to choke up. "I'll—I'll miss you, too."

"We'll call you as close to Christmas as we can, but it will depend on where we're at and if we have reception. We love you."

"I love you, too. Talk to you soon, Kate."

Nicole flipped her cell closed and tucked it away in her lab coat. She pushed her salad away and stared out the window.

"Folks going away for the holidays?"

"Yes."

"Where to?"

"A cruise along the Mexican Riviera."

"And you're not happy about that."

She straightened. "Of course I'm happy for them. Why wouldn't I be? They not only raised me, they joined the foster parent program and have helped a lot of kids find solid ground. Kate, especially, is selflessly devoted to helping children. She also took me on shortly after meeting my dad. And now, finally, they're getting away on a vacation that's just the two of them."

Damien nodded. "Why do you call her Kate instead of mother?"

He bit into his cookie as Nicole turned back to stare outside, ignoring the subject she knew he wasn't done with.

He proved her right after he finished eating. "You're upset they are leaving over the Christmas holiday."

She turned to him tight-lipped, but the simple truth stole her resolve. Nicole felt her lip quiver. "It's always been an important holiday for us to share as a family. My mother," her voice broke a little further, "loved Christmas. Dad and Kate always made sure it was a special day for me."

"So now it's time for you to create your own kind of special Christmas."

Nicole stood and slapped her half-full plate on the tray. The man was good at driving the obvious home. "Yes, Doctor. Now I get to figure out how to enjoy a holiday I love while being buried beneath an overwhelming work load and crazy hours."

She stalked off, not caring one whit what he thought. Nicole didn't get far before a hand on her arm stopped her.

"I'm sorry. My intention was not to anger you."

But you did. She stared at him for a long moment, then relented, feeling her shoulders relax as the anger drained away. "I know you didn't. I'm being way too sensitive...and selfish."

He crooked his arm and smiled. "Come on. Sit with me while I finish my coffee."

It was hard not to get pulled into those eyes, especially when they crinkled up at the edges like now. Nicole bit back a smile, but it took a tremendous effort. "All right."

He refilled her coffee cup and settled down across from her.

"How's your patient, Mary, doing?" Nicole figured patient care would be a safe topic.

"Pain's slowly diminishing, but we've got her on some pretty heavy meds to make that happen."

"Any results from the CT scan?"

"Preliminary only," he answered. "There's no indication so far of any bleeding issues, arteritis, or aneurysm."

"That's good," Nicole said with a nod.

"Very good," Damien agreed. "Except we still don't know what's causing all this. To top it all off, she's got a low grade fever now and some migratory joint pain."

Nicole frowned. "These are new symptoms?"

"Yes." Damien ran both hands through his hair and Nicole couldn't help but notice how easily he did that. She wanted to run her own hands through the wavy dark lengths. Mentally shaking herself, she focused on what he was saying.

"—not used to this. I'm a good diagnostician."

"You are," she said.

He slapped a hand on the table, their coffee slopping over the edges of the cups. "Yet I can't figure out what's wrong with this patient. I can't ease her pain."

Nicole reached out and covered his hand with hers. "You *will* figure this out. I'm certain of it."

He covered hers with his free one and they both stared at their hands, before Nicole reluctantly pulled hers away. "Have any other symptoms exhibited themselves?"

"She had what appeared to be a bout of confusion this afternoon. The migraine could explain that."

"Chronic fatigue syndrome?"

"I considered that, but it doesn't account for the photosensitivity. Plus, she jogs regularly and has no trouble recovering from that."

"Depression?"

"It doesn't fit the pattern. I've also considered eating disorders. And I've ruled out thyroid issues."

She wracked her brain for something that would encompass the wide ranging symptoms. "Fibromyalgia?"

He crooked his head. "Maybe."

Just then his pager went off. He glanced at it and jumped up. "It's Mary."

Nicole followed, barely keeping pace as he launched himself up the stairs two at a time. By the time she reached the fourth floor, she was out of breath and he was nowhere to be found. She hurried to his patient's room and found it alive with activity.

Without turning, he spoke to Nicole. "She's seizing."

She knew all they could do was help her ride it out. It took a while, but Mary's body eventually settled into an exhausted, almost comatose state.

After everyone else emptied out of the room, Damien pulled a chair close to the bed. Nicole, now off the clock, contemplated the fourteen hour reprieve she was due for. Her own bed, in an apartment she hadn't seen for several days, beckoned.

As she watched the physician she'd come to greatly admire, she knew she wouldn't be going home anytime soon. "I'll be back in a moment," she told him.

He never looked up or even acknowledged her comment.

Nicole raced to her locker and grabbed her textbook of diseases. Taking it back to the patient's room with her, she pulled a chair next to Damien's and opened the book.

It took some time to find it, but the thread of symptoms eventually led her to a possibility. "Damien?"

He must have caught the excitement in her voice because he straightened and leaned toward her. "Have you found something?"

"I think so. Although there's no telltale rash."

He stared at her.

"Damien, I think she has an auto-immune disorder. I think she has Lupus."

He remained mute, but she saw the spark of belief flare in his eyes. He glanced at the patient and then back at Nicole. "I think you've hit on it." His voice was a rushed whisper as he reached for the textbook and read. "It's all here. Joint pain, headache, even the seizure can be tied to this diagnosis."

He stood, handing her the book. "I've got to order some additional tests. And some steroids to help ease her symptoms." He strode toward the door, but quickly returned to Nicole's side, pulling her up and into his arms. "Doctor, you have earned your degree today." He gave her a quick kiss on the lips, then was out the door before she could react.

Nicole sank to the chair, her fingers gliding over lips that still felt the imprint of his. She hugged her chest, trying to hold close the warm tingle from their embrace. A slow smile spread across her face. Today was a good day.

She glanced at her watch. Tonight, actually. It was after 2A.M. and she was overdue for some sleep. As she watched the patient's chest rise and fall in measured breaths, Nicole settled into a comfortable position in the chair and wait for Damien's return.

There was really no other place she wanted to be right now than by his side.

CHAPTER SEVEN

A gentle caress filtered through the mud of deep sleep and got Nicole's attention. She curled into it, not yet ready to wake up. It grew more insistent. She brushed the touch away, but it returned.

Opening one eye, she pinpointed the irritation as Damien's grinning face came into view. She groaned as she opened up both eyes and tried to figure out where she was. This wasn't her bedroom. It was a hospital room.

It hit her as she stretched. She was still in Mary's room. Damien's patient. She looked around. The room was awash in daylight, something that had been intolerable for Mary. Yet here she was, awake, sitting up in bed, and smiling.

Nicole's lips quirked up. "You feel better," she said.

"Yes, I do," Mary said. "Not perfect, but the headache is down to a dull roar."

"We've still got a ways to go to get the inflammation down," Dr. Reed said to Mary. "But you've responded quickly and well to the initial medications. You'll need to continue under the care of a rheumatologist, but I think it's safe to say you'll be able to go home in a day or two."

"I like that idea. The best news of all is that I spoke to the head of the department my studies are in," Mary said. "I think they'll grant me a time waiver so I can still take my exams."

Nicole's grin widened. "That's great news." She stretched again, trying to ease muscles stiffened by sleeping in a chair. "How long have I been asleep?"

"About four hours," Damien said. "I didn't have the heart to wake you."

Her watch verified the time. "Well," she said, "I've still got about ten hours left before I'm back on shift. I think I'm going home to shower and change clothes." She looked down at the wrinkled khakis she'd been wearing for somewhere around thirty six hours. "These are definitely past their prime."

Damien walked her out. In the hall, he took both her hands in his. "Thank you for finding this solution. I don't know why I didn't see it."

"You would have gotten there. I didn't put the symptoms together for a long time, either. Lupus is tough to diagnose."

He nodded. "I—" He shuffled from foot to foot. When an orderly passed by them, Damien dropped her hands and stuffed his deep into his pockets. "I hope you get some more rest. You've certainly earned it."

She frowned, wondering what he had really meant to say. "I'll settle for a chance to do some laundry and eat something that's not hospital food."

Damien laughed. "I know what you mean. I can't remember the last time I had a home cooked meal."

"Well, I'm not a gourmet chef, but I know my way around a kitchen. We could celebrate with a home cooked breakfast at my place." Nicole felt the breath whoosh out of her lungs and struggled to keep from clamping a hand over her mouth. She knew she was as red as the blood rushing to her face. Had she really invited her boss, the hunky Dr. Damien Reed, over for an intimate meal for two?

"Um, I mean, um, well, I'm sorry. That was forward of me. You're my boss, after all. Forget I said that, okay?"

She would have turned and run, but he stopped her with three simple words.

"I'd love to."

She gulped, thinking of the current state of her apartment, the fact that she now needed to pick up groceries, and that she only had a few short hours to get through all this and be on shift here at the hospital. "All right."

"When and where?"

Damien's voice had dropped into the deep, quiet range she found sexy as hell and Nicole felt her hormones answer. It was going to be a long morning.

She wrote down her address for him, picked an hour that hopefully would give her enough prep time and get her back to work by her shift. As she left the hospital, she realized snow had begun to fall again in earnest. It was a good thing both the twenty-four hour grocery store and her apartment were within walking distance. She was a lousy snow driver.

A rushed three hours later her apartment had some semblance of order to it, a breakfast casserole baked away in the oven, and the smell of homemade bread filled the room. Brewing coffee dripped away and dishes were in place on the table.

Nicole stood in front of her small closet wondering what on earth she should wear for breakfast with her boss.

Her boss.

She said the words over and over again. Somewhere, over the past few days, she'd stopped thinking of him that way and that was dangerous. She didn't have time for relationships, most certainly not a complicated one that broke rules she had agreed to when entering this program. Not that it was even a possibility. There was no way Damien Reed thought of her in that way.

Nicole turned this way and that in the mirror, wondering how he saw her. Granted, she was trim, but her breasts were too small and her legs too long. She yanked a dark green turtleneck over her head, and slipped into a wool skirt. She simply did not have any "date" clothes.

As she ran a brush through her hair, she frowned, wishing she had a more vibrant hair color than mousy brown with a touch of red. Maybe when she finished her residency and actually earned a living wage, she'd have it foiled and add some blond highlights. She started to pin it up, but decided against it and let the soft curls settle around her shoulders. At least she was lucky enough to have her mother's thick hair. Getting it under control for work took some doing.

How many years had it been since someone had brushed her hair? Her mother used to style and braid it often. She'd loved those times. They had talked about everything. In her stepmother's defense, Kate had tried. Nicole remembered how much of a brat she'd been about Kate doing her hair and felt a twinge of guilt. She'd been pretty hard on her stepmother and wondered how Kate had managed to tolerate it.

Nicole was startled out of her reverie by the doorbell. She hadn't put a lick of makeup on but was officially out of time. Damien would have to take what he got.

She glanced through the peephole, a conditioned response, and her eyes widened as she saw him straightening his tie. The man didn't wear a tie at the hospital, but he wears one to breakfast with...a co-worker?

She glanced down again at her drab skirt. A debutante, she wasn't. *Oh, well.* She opened the door.

Damien picked something up from the floor and straightened. A plant. He had brought a plant? Nicole felt more confused than ever. "Hi," she said.

"Hi." He held out the poinsettia. "I brought this as a thank you."

She took it from him, hugging the pot to her chest, knowing the apartment behind her showed no holiday spirit. In fact, it looked pretty much the same as it had every other day.

"Thank you," she said, burying her face in petals she knew had no real scent. "It's very thoughtful of you."

He pulled his hand around from behind his back. "I, um, also brought this."

The bottle wasn't wine. It was maple syrup and in one of the New England states signature leaf-shaped jars. She stifled a grin, knowing she had a jar exactly like it in her closet, ready to ship to her folks for the holidays.

He cocked his head, smiling. "It's a little too touristy, isn't it?"

"It's perfect and I love it. Thank you." She motioned him in.

"I was going to bring wine as a gift, but since this is a breakfast..." The words trailed off as he set the syrup down and shrugged off his coat.

She laughed. "Wine would be good if I have to spend another day under Dr. Jones' thumb."

"Is he still giving you trouble?"

"No more than you do." Nicole's hand flew to her mouth when she realized what she'd said. "Sorry," she mumbled.

"It's just part of the service we offer as mentors, I guess," he said, laughing.

Nicole decided then and there that if making her life difficult made him laugh like this, it was worth it.

"Flaying the backs of your interns is *not* funny," she said. Her efforts at being serious failed as the corners of her mouth tugged upward.

She settled the poinsettia on the end table, turning it this way and that. He laid his coat over the arm of the couch and watched until she had it just right. With a final tap on one of the leaves, she picked up the syrup and turned back to Damien.

"You know, I could talk to Dr. Jones if you like," Damien said.

"Who's going to talk to you?"

He raised his eyebrows. "Have I really been that hard on you?"

"Yes," she shot back. "You have." She sighed, knowing that wasn't the truth. "I'll admit I think it's made me a better doctor. Thank you for that."

Damien inclined his head in acknowledgement. "So you don't want me to talk to him?"

"No." She was vehement. "He's got it in for me at the moment, but I can take care of my own problems."

"I like that about you," he said, his voice low.

Nicole felt the heat of a blush tinge her cheeks and turned away to hide it. "Breakfast is almost ready," she said.

He followed her into the kitchen which, for the first time since she moved in, felt claustrophobic.

"I like this," he said.

She looked around at the small, tangerine-colored room. "That's the idea. I needed a cheerful place."

He sniffed. "And it smells great, too."

"You may want to reserve judgment on that until you taste it." She pulled the casserole out and set it on the table.

Damien leaned over her shoulder. "It looks as good as it smells."

She nodded, unable to speak with him so close. Did it seem like he stayed there longer than was necessary? He backed away and Nicole decided it must have been her imagination. She cleared her throat. "Warm food seemed like a good choice, considering the weather."

Damien pulled back the curtain and Nicole glanced outside. Snow fell in big, white flakes. It probably wouldn't stop for hours, but this was New York. Snow didn't stop life here. It didn't even slow it down.

She set the syrup on the table. "I didn't make anything this can go with."

"It's a gift. Use it when you need to. Of course," he paused, "if it meant an invitation for another home cooked breakfast, I wouldn't be opposed."

"Ah, so you have a plan," she said, slicing the bread.

"I do have a plan," he said.

Nicole paused at the focus she heard in his voice. She didn't get the chance to question him, though, as he changed the subject.

"I didn't notice any holiday decorations."

"That's not true. There's a lovely poinsettia sitting front and center in my living room."

"But nothing else?"

"There's been no time to decorate," she said. *Translation: I spend my meager salary on food and rent instead of decorations.*

Still, the pang of a Christmas without them hit hard and Nicole sighed. Shaking her head, she set bread slices out and served up sections of the egg, potato, and sausage casserole. They sat down at the two-person table she'd nabbed from a graduating student last summer. It had always worked fine for her. Now, the area felt small and confining. Somehow, being close enough to touch knees with Damien Reed did strange things to her nervous system.

"The casserole's hot. Be careful."

He forked a bite, and then leaned in to blow gently on it. Nicole felt a tingle weave its way through her body and settle somewhere low in her stomach as she watched. His eyes met hers and he winked before popping the forkful in his mouth.

Then his eyes widened in pleasure. "This is good. Very good, in fact," he said. The look on his face said he hadn't expected that.

"Thanks for the vote of confidence." Nicole laughed.

At least he had enough humility to look sheepish. She cocked her head. The look was kind of endearing on him.

He paused mid-bite. "What?"

"Nothing," she said, focusing on her own plate.

"You had a funny look on your face," he said, grinning.

She didn't know how to answer. She'd never been one to hedge, but this...attraction was new territory for her. She opted for a piece of the truth. "I guess I'm just not used to seeing you away from the hospital."

"I like you this way." She stared at the napkin she had started to shred, wondering what cupboard she could crawl into.

The fact that Damien didn't laugh scared her more than just about anything. Instead, he covered her hand with his. "I like this, too."

Breakfast forgotten, she stared at their hands as unfamiliar warmth washed through her body and settled like a comforting blanket around her. She tried to stop her heart from overriding her mind.

When she looked up, darkened green eyes stared back at her and she knew everything she'd tried to convince herself of wasn't true. He felt it, too. She could see it reflected in those eyes.

When he leaned forward, her heart began to pound against the inside of her chest. *He's going to kiss me.*

He paused a fraction of a second from her lips. She sensed no indecision. Maybe he, like her, wanted to savor this moment. To feel it unfold like a slow ripple in time.

When their lips touched, that ripple expanded until there was nothing in her world except Damien and the paradise she felt as they kissed.

This was no hot and bothered I-need-sex-now kiss. Instead, there was a sweetness, a gentle discovery to it that wove a cocoon of joy around her heart.

When he pulled away, she could have sworn she heard a softly whispered "wow" before he sat back. She wanted to echo the sentiment. One gentle kiss and she'd fallen off the edge of a precipice. She took a deep breath, trying to slow her heartbeat.

Nicole realized she was falling for Damien Reed, something that should not be happening. It would complicate her life to no end.

"You know," he said. "We can't really date."

She knew it. It wasn't what she'd figured would be the first words out of his mouth after kissing her. Disappointed, she tried to hide it, tried to put on her poker face. There was only one problem. She'd been told again and again that she didn't have a poker face.

"But," Damien continued. "I'm not always going to be your boss."

A flicker of hope brought a slow smile to her face.

He reached again for her hand. Several long moments passed as he moved his fingers across hers. Nicole enjoyed the sensation and waited.

When he spoke, it once again was not what she'd expected to hear.

"Come spend Christmas with me," Damien said.

"Christmas?" She couldn't switch gears that fast.

"Yes. At my home, well, my parent's home. Come spend it with us."

"With you...*and* your folks?"

His lips moved upwards in a lopsided grin. "Yes. I'm asking you to spend Christmas with my parents, my sister and brother-in-law, and myself."

"I-I'm not sure I can get it off. I volunteered to work when I found out I wasn't going home."

He shook his head. "I think your boss can figure out a way."

"Oh! We can't...I mean...you *are* my boss. We're not supposed to..."

He placed a finger on her lips to silence her. "There's nothing in the rules that says I can't invite a co-worker home for a holiday meal. You did mention that Christmas is a special time of year for you, right?"

Nicole remembered their conversation in the cafeteria. That's what he was doing. Taking pity on her. "I don't need you to make my Christmas happy. I'm a big girl and I can take care of myself."

He pulled her hand up to his lips and kissed her palm and she suppressed the shiver of desire that raised the hair on the back of her neck.

"Trust me. I am fully aware of how grown up you are, Nicole Milbourne. I do, however, have no doubt that you will work the entire holiday and try very hard to forget that it's Christmas. Come home with me. I know it won't be the same as with your folks, and I don't know what memories you hold from holidays with your mother, but I bet you'll enjoy my family."

She wavered. She really didn't want to spend Christmas with strangers. Damien did so much out of the goodness of his heart and her mind said that was his reason for inviting her. Her heart prayed there were other, more personal reasons.

"Come because your mother would want you to," he said.

His eyes held hers and she found herself unable to look away. Nicole fought the rush of emotion his gaze brought on. Damien Reed knew too much about her. He knew what buttons to push. What he didn't know was that she hesitated not because of the idea of spending Christmas with strangers. She didn't want to spend Christmas with a man she was falling for with and couldn't have.

He squeezed her hand. "Please?"

"All right," she said. "Thank you for inviting me."

"Good." With that matter settled, Damien attacked his breakfast with relish and the conversation returned to work and superficial topics.

After they finished breakfast and the dishes, Damien waited for her to change and walked her back to the hospital in time for her shift.

"We shouldn't be seen together."

"Why? We're co-workers."

"No. We're not. You're my boss and people will talk."

"Let them. We've done nothing against the rules." They'd reached the emergency room doors and stopped. She wanted to reach out and touch him. To feel his warmth one more time before they returned fully back to their peer relationship. His hand came up as if he wanted to do the same thing, but he tucked both hands into his jeans instead.

"Thanks for the breakfast, Dr. Milbourne. It was," his voice deepened, "exceptional."

Nicole couldn't tear her eyes away from his lips. She followed his lead and stuck her hands deep into her coat pockets before she gave into the urge to grab the lapels of his jacket and pull him to her.

She saw one of the nurses watching from inside. "I'd better go."

Damien nodded. "I'll work out the schedules and let you know."

She thought about protesting the invitation one last time, but clamped her mouth shut, knowing he expected her to argue. "All right," she said.

As she walked away, she knew she'd capitulated not because he'd won, or because she had no other alternative.

She'd given in because, in her heart, she very much wanted to go.

CHAPTER EIGHT

A solid week went by with little or no conversation between Damien and herself, other than patient care. Nicole's last nerve was just about gone. Had he decided inviting her home was a mistake? She yanked her lab coat on and headed for Amanda Grant's room.

"Hi, Amanda," Nicole said, working hard to bury her worry and focus on her friend. Since Amanda had been diagnosed with ovarian cancer, the two of them had re-forged a friendship Nicole treasured. The rules stated Nicole couldn't be Amanda's physician, but that didn't stop her from making sure everything looked all right.

She grabbed the chart and dropped into a chair next to the bed. "How are you feeling?"

"Oh, you know," her friend answered. "I've been better." Amanda kept steady eyes on Nicole. Gentle eyes that seemed larger with the absence of most of her hair.

Nicole silently agreed. Her friend looked like she'd spent a year in hell. She'd lost weight. There were deep circles under her eyes. And her skin had turned almost translucent.

She should have rebounded from her last chemotherapy session by now. Nicole opened the chart. Her lab work cleared her for this next chemo session. Just barely. Her numbers were down, but not alarmingly low.

She flipped through the chart. "You should be feeling better than this. I don't understand why you haven't recovered more."

A hand touched Nicole's arm and she glanced up, seeing a quiet resolve in Amanda's eyes that was unsettling. She swallowed. Her friend looked like a woman on a mission. A very sick woman on a mission. Nicole rubbed her arms. Had it gotten chilly in here?

"We need to talk," Amanda said.

An instinct for preservation kicked into high gear and whispered "run" to Nicole. She glanced at her watch. "I'm due on shift in a few minutes. I can come by during lunch."Nicole stood. "I really should get moving. I did want to wish you good luck with today's chemotherapy."

Nicole made it to the end of the bed before the bomb fell in the form of Amanda Grant's soft voice. "I'm not going to have chemotherapy."

Nicole flipped open the chart to the med list. There they were. All the cancer-killing meds were ordered, as well as the palliative medications to help her through the next several days. She looked up. "What do you mean--?"

"I've decided to stop chemotherapy."

"You mean delay it until you feel better."

"No. I mean stop it."

"But that's a...a..."

"Death sentence. I know."

Nicole felt the walls start to close in. She stepped closer. "You can't do this. You're tired. Give it some time. You can't just give up."

"For what? For a few more weeks? Or months? I have stage four cancer. You, above all people, know how bad that is."

Tears pooled in Nicole's eyes and she blinked to clear her vision. "I also know you can't give up hope. They could come up with a breakthrough any day. Even any moment. You haven't given chemotherapy a chance. A couple rounds isn't enough to slow things down."

"No, it's not. But it is enough for me to recognize what my quality of life will be."

While Nicole grew more upset, she saw Amanda's resolve remain constant and that panicked her more than anything. She grasped her friend's hand. "Amanda, I haven't known you long, but I know you're a strong woman. An amazing woman.

You're too young to make this kind of decision. You have a lot still to do. Remember all the places you said you wanted to visit? Please. You can't quit."

Amanda pulled her hand out and placed it on top of Nicole's. "I've been through this before, remember? I watched my mother go through all these treatments." She paused before continuing, gripping Nicole's hand tighter. "I know you had a rough time with your mother, Nicole."

"That's got nothing to do with this."

"I think it does. It colors decisions you make when you're close to a situation, like now." She took a deep breath. "You know what I wish. I wish you could be at peace with your mother's death. I want that more than anything for you, my friend. I've seen how good you are at what you do. I've seen you learn what you can give to the world. Now you need to learn how to receive. How to let others into your heart like you've let me in."

Nicole bit her lip to keep from crying. "It hurts too much to let people in."

Amanda nodded. "Sometimes it does hurt. But there's a flip side. A wonderful one that more than compensates for any pain."

Nicole knew there was some truth in what Amanda said, but her heart couldn't handle it. "I—I can't let you do this, Amanda."

"It's not your decision to make. I'm going home, Nicole."

"Today?" She stared at her, confused. "You're being discharged?"

"I'll be in here a couple days for more tests. After that I'm going back to California. I grew up there. I've spoken to my brother and his wife. They want me to come and live with them."

"But that means—"

"We may not see each other again." Amanda's eyes filled with tears. "I hate that part of this decision. You are what I will miss the most. I'm sorry. I don't want to spend what time I have left looking at snow. I want warmth and sunshine."

Tears streamed freely down Nicole's face now. She was being deserted all over again. And there wasn't a thing she could do about it.

Nicole stood and, with supreme effort, found her emotional equilibrium. "I guess, if that's the way you feel about it, there's nothing I can do to change your mind."

"Nicole, I don't want us to part this way. It's not good for either of us, but most especially you. Don't retreat into your shell. You've got a whole new life opening up in front of you. Embrace it."

Nicole swiped at the tears on her face. "Don't worry about me. I'll be just fine. I wish you—" She couldn't say the word peace. It stuck in her throat like salt on a wound. With a gasp, she whirled and fled the room.

And ran smack into Dr. Damien Reed.

He gripped her by the shoulders and steered her into an empty waiting room.

"I'm so sorry, Nicole," he said, pulling her against his chest.

She didn't want his sympathy. She didn't want him to feel bad for her. Or for Amanda. She wanted him to fight. She wanted to fight for Amanda's life.

She pulled back and thumped his chest. "How can she make this choice? She doesn't know what she's doing."

She kept pounding. After several long moments, she collapsed against him. "Why? Why is she doing this?"

"Can you understand that she wants to enjoy what time she has left?"

"But she could double, even triple her time with chemotherapy. Maybe even go into remission."

"The chances of that happening are pretty slim with her diagnosis." He pulled her chin up. "You know that."

She sniffed. "Stranger things have happened. She can't just give up."

"She's not giving up. She's making a choice, empowering herself and taking control of the time she has left."

Nicole heard him. She understood what he was saying, but she couldn't grasp the idea with her heart. "You are better at separating your feelings from things like patient choices. You sound like you've been through this with patients before."

"Once or twice."

The feeling that she was missing something kept nagging at her. She pulled back and looked at him. And saw the truth. "You counseled Amanda, didn't you?"

He hesitated, and then gave a quick nod of his head.

"You convinced her to give up."

"You know me better than that. I only answered her questions as best I could. She made the decision on her own."

"But you *agree* with her choice."

"I *respect* her choice. There's a difference."

Nicole shook her head. "No. There's not. At least, not for me. I would never agree to someone giving up. My mother never gave up. She fought to the end."

"Are you sure about that? Is it possible a ten year-old, well-loved daughter might have been shielded from some of the worst of her mother's disease? From some of the choices she made?"

"My. Mother. Never. Gave. Up. And I cannot—*will* not condone anyone's choice to stop fighting." Nicole swiped at lingering tears on her cheek, stood tall and straightened her lab coat. "If you'll excuse me, Dr. Reed, I'm due on shift."

"Don't do this, Nicole," he said, placing a hand on her arm. "Don't shut yourself off again."

She shrugged him off. "It's the only way I know how to survive, Doctor." She walked out of the room wondering if her legs would carry her. Ducking into the nearest restroom, she slammed the stall door shut and crumpled onto the floor.

Damn it all to hell. It was happening all over again. Someone she cared about was dying and there wasn't a thing she could do about it. Nicole leaned back against the stall door and hugged herself, closing her eyes tight against the tears.

Why had she become a doctor if she couldn't save the people who were important to her? Why? Everything felt muddled together. Amanda's choice, Damien's acceptance, visions of her mother in those last few months.

The bathroom felt hot, stifling, confining. Nicole needed out. Out of this hospital. Away from this way of life where she'd believed she could actually help people.

She ran into the hallway. Damien leaned against the wall, waiting for her. She shook her head. "I can't talk to you now."

"Don't shut me out. Let me help."

Nicole signaled with her hand for him to stop. "I don't want to talk to any doctors right now. Least of all, you."

Nicole ran toward the E.R. and out through the doors. She trudged through the snow in work shoes and lab coat, having left her winter coat back in her locker. It only took a couple of blocks for the sub-freezing temperature to take hold and chill her through.

Nicole dug in her pockets and realized she didn't even have her apartment key. She glanced back toward the hospital and knew she wasn't ready to return there.

A few doors down, she came to the local public library. Hurrying inside, she kept going until she was between bookshelves as far back as she could go. Nicole squatted against the wall, hugging herself like her arms were the only thing keeping her body from exploding, and waited for the shivers to die down.

It took several minutes before her teeth stopped chattering and she could stand without spasms of phantom cold coursing through her body. Even more time passed before she truly felt warm again.

No matter how hard she tried, or how numb she wanted to be, she couldn't run from it any longer.

Is it possible your mother shielded you from the worst of it?

No. She would not have done that. Would she?

I respect Amanda's decision.

But it's not the right one. Is it?

Don't do this, Nicole. Don't shut me out.

I have to. You're helping my friend die. Or...are you?

Nicole winced. Her mind knew she was being unfair. The problem was how to get that through to her heart.

Did my mother shield me? She grabbed a book, any book, and sat down in an overstuffed chair in the corner. She opened the book on her lap, but the words blurred as she thought about her mother's death. She'd been ten at the time. She remembered hearing her mother at night, trying to hide how sick she was. She remembered creeping into the bathroom, getting a washcloth for her mother, rubbing her back, anything to make the hurt go away.

Then she remembered all the extra times she'd gone to her father's to stay. And the sleepovers with friends.

Maybe her mother had tried to keep the worst of her disease from Nicole. But she'd done session after session of chemotherapy. She'd fought to the end.

Nicole had seen death a time or two since starting her residency. She'd seen the look on patients' faces when the time came. The look of despair on their faces changed to acceptance and, finally, a sort of peace.

She could no longer deny that her mother must have gone through those same emotions. Maybe there had been a point when she'd said enough. When she'd decided it was okay to leave.

Except she left me. Just like Amanda was doing now.

Nicole shook her head. This wasn't about her. She wasn't the one dying. Amanda had the right to make her own decisions.

She hung her head. *Just like my mother did.*

And I didn't make it any easier. That, however, was a wrong Nicole could make right. She closed the book and, for the first time, read the title and chuckled.

The Healing Season: a Christmas to Remember.

Glancing skyward, she wondered how any force could be working so hard to heal her wounds. Wounds she'd never tried to heal by herself until now. She placed the book back on the shelf, saw the time on her watch, and the bottom dropped back out of her world. She'd been gone for hour s...while she was supposed to be on duty.

That was a violation of the worst kind. An offense that could mean instant dismissal from the program. Her heart raced faster than her feet as she rushed through the library. She needed to be back at the hospital now.

"Excuse me, miss?"

The voice stopped her. She turned to see a man behind the checkout desk holding out a coat?

"A man dropped this off a while ago. Pointed you out and said to leave you alone, but you'd need this eventually.

Damien! Her hands flew to her face. She'd said some horrible things to him. He'd never forgive her. She threw her arms into the coat, paused to take a long, fortifying whiff of his scent and, with a thank you tossed over her shoulder, rushed out the door.

By the time she arrived at the hospital, her shoes were once again soaked. There was no time to change now. She tossed Damien's coat behind the triage counter and went in search of him.

Before she found him, Dr, Jones found her. "Where have you been, Dr. Milbourne?"

Oh, crap. This was the nail that would seal her fate. Nicole couldn't come up with a single reason to explain her absence. The only thing to do was to come clean and pray the man had some shred of decency in him.

"I—"

"Dr. Milbourne has been out of the facility on a research project I asked her to follow up on."

Nicole whirled around to see Damien, certain her eyes were about to bug out of her head.

"Are you certain that's the story you want to go with, Dr. Reed? I have witnesses who saw her run out of the hospital in an agitated state. If you are lying, you could lose your accreditation and, with that, everything you've worked for the last few years."

No. Nicole couldn't, and wouldn't, let Damien put his own career on the line for her. She turned back to the attending physician. "I was out of the hospital, Dr. Jones. This is not Dr. Reed's fault."

"There is no fault here," Damien said. "Dr. Milbourne took time I granted to come to terms with a difficult diagnosis."

"No. I left on personal business," she said, turning to glare at him.

"No. You didn't. It was sanctioned time away," he said, locking eyes with her.

"Enough!" They both turned to Dr. Jones. He stood there with lips compressed for several endless seconds. Nicole stuck her hands deep in her hospital coat pockets, crossing fingers on both and praying for leniency.

"I'm not sure what's gone on here today." He shook his head. "And since you two are more interested in saving the other than telling me, I'm going to have to make a decision based on what I know."

Here it comes. All the hard work, the studying, making the dean's list...it was all about to go down the tube. She felt Damien take a step closer, but he didn't touch her. He must know if he did, she'd explode, as keyed up as she was.

"What I know is that each of you has shown abilities beyond your studies."

The ringing in Nicole's ear wouldn't stop and she was having trouble understanding Dr. Jones as he continued.

"I know that you have also both shown exemplary concern for your patients."

That got through. The man was paying both of them a compliment?

"I believe—" He got a pained look on his face. "—that you will both turn out to be excellent physicians in your respective fields. And, since patient care was not at risk, I think we'll consider this matter settled."

He turned to leave and Nicole's shoulders edged down toward normal. Before Dr. Jones got too far away to be heard, he turned back. "Don't let this happen again."

"No, sir." Nicole and Damien answered at the same time.

Nicole watched him until he was out of sight, then turned to Damien. She could see wariness in his eyes and in his straight stance.

"Thank you," she said.

"No problem."

"Um, we need to talk."

He nodded his head.

"But there's someone else I need to talk to first."

His voice softened. "Yes. Go. You and I—" he pointed a finger at each of them, "—have lots of time."

Nicole stopped outside Amanda's room to brace herself. This would, most likely, be the hardest thing she would ever do. She was going to say goodbye.

Right after she apologized profusely for her horrible behavior. She straightened her shoulders and pushed the door open.

Amanda Grant wasn't alone. A man close to her in age, and with the same auburn color to his hair, stood near the window.

"Oh, I'm sorry. You've got company," Nicole said. "I'll come back later."

"No," Amanda answered right away. "Stay. I'd like you to meet my brother, James."

As they shook hands, Amanda told James that Nicole had kept her sane through these past few weeks. Nicole shook her head, trying to deny it.

"You have been my ally and friend," Amanda told her. She turned to James. "Could you give us a few minutes?"

"Sure. I could use a cup of good coffee, anyhow. The stuff out of the machines isn't much more than badly flavored water."

"Don't I know it," Nicole said.

After he left, Nicole wasted no time. "I'm so sorry."

"No need to apologize. I kind of blindsided you."

"No. You have every right to make the choice that is best for you."

"Yes. But maybe I could have told you in a gentler way."

"And maybe I could have listened to what you were really saying," Nicole said. "I'm a doctor. And part of my training has been to learn how important listening is." A vision of Damien's approving face brought the edge of a smile to Nicole's.

She sat on Amanda's bed and reached for her hand. "I don't know what I'll do without you around to be my sounding board. Who will right my world when Dr. Jones tosses me to the wolves?"

"You'll do just fine. You already have. And don't think my moving to California lets you off the hook. I expect regular updates on how things are going with Dr. Tall, Dark, and Handsome."

"Dr...what?"

"You heard me."

"He's my boss," Nicole said.

Amanda chortled. "He's way more than your boss. I see it in both your eyes. You're in love with the man. And if you don't act on it and snap him up before someone else does, I may just come back and haunt you."

This was the one topic Nicole had kept close to her heart. How could Amanda possibly know? And if she knew, did anyone else?

"The whole hospital is buzzing about you two."

"Oh, no!" A crimson blush heated Nicole's cheeks. "It can't be so," she said.

Amanda laughed. "Oh, yes, sister. A lot of hearts are breaking in this place. They've all come to the easy-to-reach conclusion that Dr. Damien Reed is off the market."

"How will I ever face any of them?"

"With your head held high, that's how."

"He's, um, invited me to spend Christmas with his family."

"You are going, right? You *have* to go, Nicole." Amanda grabbed her arms. "You and I both know from personal experience how fleeting life is. You need to grab happiness while you can. Your mother would want you to."

Nicole felt the bittersweet in her smile. "Yes, she would."

"Then say you'll go. Please."

Nicole nodded. "I'll go."

Amanda settled back into her pillow and nodded. "Good. I think this is going to become another one of your favorite holiday memories."

Nicole had a strong feeling her friend was right.

CHAPTER NINE

"I can't believe I never asked how far it was."

Now that they were on their way, a serious case of doubt tied Nicole's stomach up in acid-dipped knots. She wrapped her purse strap around her finger, unwound it, and then wound it again.

"Why didn't you mention it was a two-day drive?"

He flashed the lopsided smile that generally got him what he wanted. "Because I knew you wouldn't come with me if I told you. Besides, it's only a day's drive when there's no snow on the ground."

She glanced outside at the white landscape. "So you wait until we are well on our way to tell me this?"

He shrugged, exhibiting not one ounce of remorse. "I waited until turning back would be difficult."

"I have only five days off at the hospital, you know."

"I know. I booked you out. And it wasn't easy, since you'd cancelled your days off. Still, I could have worked it out for seven, or even six days instead of just the five. It would have made it easier."

The memory of yesterday's goodbye with Amanda added to the sour taste in her mouth. She'd looked so at peace, but Nicole knew how bleak Amanda's future was. How could she take this time away when cancer had such a hold on so many people?

"I didn't go to medical school to make life easier for myself, Damien. I went to learn...to stop the disease that claimed my mother's life and now threatens Amanda. I'm here so the Amandas of the world don't have to get what amounts to a death sentence anymore."

Nicole wrung her purse strap even tighter. What was she doing here? She should be back at the hospital, finishing her residency.

Damien glanced at her sideways, sighed, and pulled over to the shoulder. Turning toward her, he stretched an arm across the back of her seat and, with the other one, gently disentangled her hand from her purse.

"I know you want to cure the world. And I applaud your determination to make that happen. But you can't live your life for research, Nicole. There has to be more."

He paused. "Are you really that upset this has become a two-day trip? Because we can turn around and go back."

He sat so still Nicole couldn't even see his chest moving. Was he holding his breath?

Did she want to go back? She should. There was so much to do. Yet the idea of this time away with Damien had worked it's way into her heart. It felt just as important. Nicole glanced back at the road that stretched out behind them. Yes, she should go back to the hospital. But that wasn't what Damien had asked her. And he had earned her honesty.

"No," she answered. "I don't want to go back."

Damien closed his eyes for a brief moment, then the lines around them crinkled up in that way she'd come to love. He touched her cheek. "I'm glad."

His touch drained any last vestige of guilt she felt at taking this time for herself. She didn't know where this thing between them was going, but she knew she wanted to follow its path, almost more than anything. Not that it didn't scare her. Nothing had ever derailed her goals before Damien Reed came along. Now here she was, heading to Vermont to spend Christmas with his family.

Damien pulled back on the road, got up to speed, and set the cruise control. Then he reached for her hand, pulling it over to his leg and holding it there.

Nicole could imagine no other place she wanted to be at that moment. Tomorrow was Christmas Eve and spending it with Damien felt like a dream come true.

They stopped to eat in a roadside café. When they got back on the road, snow had started to fall again and the wind had a definite howl to it.

"I'm not sure how much further we'll get the way this is blowing," Damien said. White knuckles on the steering wheel belied his casual tone.

Nicole chewed her lower lip. Snow in Seattle was mostly non-existent unless you drove to the mountains. She'd never traveled any distance in it and she didn't know how he could even see out the window.

"Is this a blizzard?"

Damien chuckled. "Hardly. But it is getting treacherous." He glanced at the highway sign. "I had hoped to get further today but it would be wise for us to stop."

Nicole gulped. "Whatever you think."

"I know a nice little inn a short way from the highway off this next exit. How about we stop there for the night?"

"Sounds good."

It took another half-hour of nail-biting, slow driving for them to navigate their way to the inn. Once inside, it was Nicole's turn to hold her breath. Would he order one room or two?

When he dangled two keys in front of her, she felt palpable relief, along with another, more elusive emotion. Did she want to share a room with him? She shook her head at the new feeling. She'd never...well, there had just never been much time for relationships.

"What?"

"Hmmm?"

"What did you shake your head for?"

She blushed red and mumbled something she hoped sounded like "nothing" as she turned away. He showed her to her room on the second floor and opened the door.

Nicole stared in amazement. The place was larger than her apartment. And a lot better appointed, although not in a pretentious way. An overstuffed couch sat in front of a gas fireplace. Damien flipped the switch to light it and the room felt instantly warmer. Landscapes reminiscent of the northeastern territory dotted walls accented in different shades of beige.

Nicole turned to Damien. "I can't afford this."

He waved a hand. "It's my treat."

She started to shake her head, but he stopped her with a hand on her shoulder. "Please. Let me give you this. Consider it an early Christmas present."

She stared at green eyes that fascinated her, with their myriad of colors. She could get lost in those eyes. She *was* lost in them. And probably would be for the rest of her life.

The thought brought her up short. This was not good. They'd only just begun to know each other. No way could she afford to start thinking about lifetimes.

"All right. Thank you," she finally said.

She was rewarded with a smile.

"Good. Now, is there anything you need?"

She waved a hand around the room. "What else could I possibly need?"

Damien leaned down to whisper in her ear. "Me?" He'd said it so quietly she wondered if she had heard right.

As he backed away, he asked if she was hungry, which she wasn't.

"Then why don't we take some time to relax and meet up for drinks in—" Damien glanced at his watch. "About two hours?"

Nicole nodded, her mouth too dry to formulate words. When he leaned down and kissed her lightly on the lips, her legs stopped responding to her orders and shook like she'd just finished a marathon.

She closed the door and leaned against it, her hand covering her stomach to silence the nerves doing flip flops there. She was acting like a virgin, for crying out loud.

She pushed off the door. Hell, she didn't even know if he had any intention, or any interest, in making love with her. Nicole wandered into the bathroom, delighted with the large jetted tub, separate shower and sheer tiled expanse of the room. This bathroom was bigger than her kitchen. She started the tub filling, added some hotel bath salts, and soon settled into the sudsy water.

With closed eyes, she tried to shut out the world. Instead, Damien's kiss took front and center stage. His lips, both gentle and strong, had felt tentative against hers. Searching. As if he didn't know how she would respond.

She felt her response even now deep inside. What would this night hold? And did she want to take this step? She sat up as she remembered. He was the lead resident and it was against the rules to fraternize.

She could be tossed out of the program. Everything she'd been working so hard for would be lost. She had come close to being dismissed once already. She splashed her hands in the water.

She couldn't do it. Even if he wanted to, she couldn't take the chance.

Nicole decided the only thing to do was call him and cancel their meeting for drinks. After hurriedly drying off, she wrapped the towel around her and picked up the phone by her bed.

Except she didn't know his room number. Holding the phone against her chest, she wondered if the front desk could put her through. He wouldn't be happy when she cancelled. After all, she would be spending the next couple days with his family. It would be very rude of her to simply call and cancel.

No, she decided. She'd meet him. And explain in clear terms that she could not jeopardize her career over some dalliance, some minor attraction that would more than likely disappear with the melting snow.

Nicole nodded her head and put the phone back in its cradle. Yes, that was the right thing to do.

She took special pains with make-up she rarely wore.

She sprayed perfume, a gift from her parents, in the air and let it settle over her. Mmmmm. It smelled like a light spring bouquet.

She dug through her small suitcase, tossing clothes on the bed. Nothing felt right for letting a man down easy. Especially a man who fit into his clothes like they were a comfortable second skin.

Finally she settled on the quintessential little black dress. It was demure, with a higher, slightly draping neckline. That it had a bit of sass in a backside that dipped to show no bra was incidental.

That it hugged her hips was lost on her as she enjoyed the swirl of a skirt that fell to mid-calf. Yes, this would work. She looked good in it, but not sexy. Different from work, but not saying come hither.

As she brushed her teeth, she didn't worry about the fact that she took an extra minute or two to make sure they sparkled. She applied a newly purchased lipstick and pursed her lips, well satisfied with both the color and the outline. She had nice lips.

Kissable lips.

Lips that wanted to be kissed.

Nicole sighed, knowing she had to shut that door hard. She glanced at her watch and realized she still had twenty minutes before they were to meet in the hotel bar.

She flipped through a magazine left on the desk, but found nothing of interest. She re-packed her clothes. After all, they would be leaving early in the morning.

Still fifteen minutes to go.

She straightened the bathroom.

Twelve minutes.

Deciding it was crazy to just stand here and wait, she clutched her purse and went on down to the bar.

A tree twinkled with white lights in the corner. Nicole smiled. Tomorrow would be Christmas Eve. Her second favorite day of the year. She sat in a booth where she could gaze at the tree, not minding that it felt secluded and dark.

When the waiter asked her what she wanted to drink, she opted to wait for Damien to order. She set her purse on the table, but soon moved it to her lap.

Taking a deep breath, she tried to formulate how she would tell Damien that they could only be friends. The lights on the tree twinkled away and a wave of nostalgia hit her. Her mother had loved this holiday. Kate and her Dad had, too. She missed them.

This would be such a different Christmas. She was falling in love with a man she couldn't love. Her parents were in the Caribbean. Nicole felt more alone than she had since they'd dropped her off at the airport in Seattle to head out for this residency. She wiped an errant tear from her face just as a hand settled on her shoulder. She didn't jump. She knew it was Damien.

He sat down beside her. Maybe a little too close for friends, but it felt nice so Nicole let it slide for the moment.

"Thinking about your mother?" The question, in his deep, mellow voice, didn't cause the usual rush of emotions she worked so hard to stifle.

"Is it silly to still miss her so much after all these years?"

He settled an arm around her shoulders and Nicole allowed it. After all, he was simply trying to make her feel better. That it felt so good was secondary.

"Doesn't seem that way to me," he answered. "I can't imagine what it would be like to lose a parent so young." He pulled her in tighter for a moment. "I don't want to imagine it at any age."

"I understand that better than I want to."

"It had to be hard. You were ten, right?"

"Yes. I still remember it like it was yesterday."

"Were you there?"

"No." Nicole gave a quick shake of her head. "And I held that against my dad and my grandmother for a long time afterwards."

The waiter set their drinks on the table, red wine for her and some sort of mixed drink for him. She looked at him.

"You were focused on your own memories when I got here. That was pretty obvious." He shrugged. "I took a chance you were a red wine kind of woman and ordered a cabernet I like."

He'd guessed right. She nodded and took a sip. "It's good."

He smiled, and any lingering sadness left Nicole. "Thank you," she said, looking up at him.

"You're welcome."

The strains of holiday music started up and Nicole realized there was a trio in a shadowed corner of the lounge playing music. A couple moved onto the dance floor, close together, and swayed to the slow tune.

Damien nodded toward the floor. "Let's dance."

Nicole shook her head. "I'd rather not."

"Why not?"

"I can't dance."

"Everyone says that. Come on. I promise I won't laugh...or even groan if you step on my foot."

Nicole chuckled. "All right. But don't say I didn't tell you so."

Damien stood and held out his hand. When she took it, they both paused for a moment to stare at their intertwined fingers. Nicole wondered if he felt the same heat flowing through his body as she did.

"Nice dress," he said, his eyes shining with approval.

When Nicole reached the dance floor, she turned to find Damien several steps away. He looked like he had stopped in his tracks. His mouth wasn't outright hanging open, but it was certainly slack. What had caused this reaction?

He regrouped and joined her, cocooning her hand in his as she placed her free hand on his shoulder. When his other hand settled low on her back, she felt invisible fingers of desire wrap around her and settle between her legs. She looked up at him.

Damien's eyes were dark and filled with a smoky desire. "That's—" He cleared his throat and started over. "That's a very nice dress you're wearing."

"Thank you," Nicole said.

"I've never seen you wear anything like this before."

"It's not exactly hospital wear," she said with a laugh.

"No," Damien answered. "It's much...sexier."

Sexier? This wasn't sexier. She hadn't meant to make that impression. Disconcerted, she hid her face in his chest and let him carry them around the floor in a slow cadence with the song being played. She'd never been able to dance well before. With him, it felt effortless.

That was the moment she stepped on his toe. She backed up and apologized.

Damien wasted no time pulling her back into his embrace. "See. No injuries. I think we can survive the two left feet you say you have."

"All right. But don't say I didn't warn you."

Nicole settled her cheek on his chest and gave herself up to the music...and the feel of being in Damien Reed's arms. She felt protected. And, if she was honest with herself, she liked it.

His hand crept up until it rested on the bare skin of her back and all thought fled. He moved his fingers in small motions that were anything but soothing. A warmth spread through her, becoming a heat she was having trouble ignoring.

Was he as affected as she was by this closeness?

As if reading her mind, he pulled her even tighter in to his body and she could feel his hard need. She looked up at him, her eyes wide open with a desire she could no longer hide.

At that moment the music stopped. The problem was, she hadn't stopped. Her body raged with desire for Damien. This would not do. She gave herself a mental shake and pulled away.

"We need to talk."

"I think we may be beyond talking." He reached for her as the strains of yet another mellow song wafted from the stage.

Nicole put both hands on his chest, trying hard to ignore the taut muscles she felt underneath the crisp white shirt and tie. The man looked great in jeans. In slacks and tie, he looked devastating.

Back at their table, he moved next to her, but she put some distance between them, steeling herself against the confusion in his face. She took a sip of her wine and dove in. "We can't be," she waved between them, "like this."

"Like what?"

Was the man toying with her?

"Like this," she said again. "Linked. Romantically."

His brows knit together. "Why not?"

She sighed and took another sip. "You have to understand. All I've ever wanted to do is go into medicine. I want to find cures for the cancers that steal people's lives. I have to."

"Because of your mom," he said.

"Yes. And Amanda, too. And every other woman who hears the harsh reality of the words 'ovarian cancer'. It's a vocation for me. I can't let go of that."

"There's nothing stopping you from continuing."

Oh, yes, there is. She stared into her glass, wondering how to get him to understand. "You and I dating...it can't happen. I'm so very grateful to you for everything. For your tutelage, for your patience, for inviting me to your family Christmas. But you know the rules about fraternization as well as I do."

The grin was back. "Yes," he said. "I do."

So this—" She motioned again back and forth between them. "—can't happen."

Damien nodded. "Is our working relationship the only reason?"

"Isn't it a good enough one?"

He scooted a little closer to her. "Do you mean you have no other objection to...fraternizing with me, except for work rules."

Nicole grew wary. "That's a pretty significant reason."

He moved closer still. "It would be except for one small flaw in your logic, Dr. Milbourne."

Nicole gulped. "What's that?" She whispered the words as his lips hovered mere inches from hers.

"I'm no longer in the program," he said, his eyes focused on her lips.

"What—what do you mean?"

"I mean, Doctor, that I graduated as of two days ago."

"You...graduated?" She couldn't stop staring.

His grin widened for a moment. "I knew I'd met the program requirements. Did that a couple months ago. I've stayed on...to help out."

"You have? You did?" She frowned, trying to focus on what he was saying.

"Two days ago, I met with Dr. Jones and asked to be formally graduated from the program. He accepted my resignation. So you see, work is no longer an issue between us."

"It isn't?"

She licked her lips and Damien reached up to run a finger across them. "So soft, so kissable. May I kiss you, Dr. Milbourne? May I kiss you the way I've wanted to since I first set eyes on you, fresh and green into the program."

That was when it all sunk into Nicole's conscious mind. He was free of the program. And they were free to explore each other, to see where this thing between them would go.

Could he kiss her? A slow smile spread across her face. "Oh, yes. I'd like that very much, Dr. Reed."

"Please," he said as he touched her lips. "Call me Damien."

CHAPTER TEN

One tentative touch. That's all it took for them to realize the crowded bar was no longer where either of them wanted to be. That first taste became an instant aphrodisiac and Nicole wanted more.

Much more.

Yet when she would have rushed to their room, Damien strolled. She had to admit that her arm linked in his while they waited for the elevator felt nice. It felt comfortable, like she belonged there.

Once in the elevator, he covered her hand with his. "Are you certain you want to do this?"

"Oh, yes," she said, reaching with tiptoes to pull him down for a long, lingering kiss. "More than anything."

Damien wove his free arm into her hair, pulling her closer.

"Ahem."

They broke apart, seeing the doors open and an elderly gentleman standing there waiting.

Both Nicole and Damien mumbled apologies as they traded places with the man.

"No apologies needed. Have fun," he said with a twinkle in his eyes.

The doors closed and they both burst into laughter.

Damien recovered first. "I haven't been caught making out in, well, a long, long time."

"That's a new one for me, too," Nicole said, wiping her eyes.

Damien ran a finger along her face. "You've smeared your makeup."

Oh no. Nicole's hand flew to her face. "I must look crazy."

Damien lifted her chin. "You look beautiful."

Nicole shook her head, unable to speak.

When Damien spoke again, there was a sense of awe in his voice. "You really don't know how beautiful you are, do you?"

She felt the blush and knew it was visible when he smiled.

"Come on. Let's get that stuff off your face."

Once inside her hotel room, Damien lifted her up to sit on the bathroom counter. Then, using a warm washcloth, he gently wiped the cosmetics off her face.

"Absolutely beautiful," he murmured, as if talking to himself. Then, he combed his fingers through her long hair. "You don't know how many times I wanted to pull the pins out of that bun you always wear. To see this gorgeous hair fall around your shoulders and to run my fingers through it."

Nicole sighed as he massaged her head. This felt better than, well, just about anything. He leaned in and kissed her forehead, then moved to her temple. With his hands still tangled in her hair, his lips wandered down her face. By the time he reached the corner of her lips, Nicole couldn't stand it anymore and turned to meet him.

A touch of whiskey enhanced the spicy flavor of Damien Reed. She opened her lips to taste more of him, letting her tongue reach for more.

Wrapping her arms and legs around him, she pulled him in tighter, moving her arms up and down his back, enjoying the muscles that moved as he tilted her head back to reach her neck. It took very little to un-tuck his shirt and feather touches along the beltline of his slacks had him groaning.

He straightened, Nicole coming with him as he renewed their kiss. She wrapped her arms tightly around him as he moved and she soon felt the bed underneath her.

Damien leaned over her, an arm on either side, and kissed her again. Then he moved to lie beside her. She reached for him, but he stopped her. Instead of kissing her lips, he pulled the draped material away from her shoulder and began to pepper kisses along her collarbone.

Nicole felt the brand of each kiss and welcomed it.

When he drew her dress down further and Nicole knew no bra stood in their way, she began to chew her lip. She'd never been, um, amply endowed. Would she be enough?

He glanced up and smiled. "You are everything I dreamed you would be."

Nicole gulped, and then returned his smile with one of her own. He kissed her then, and she melted against him. When he moved to the still-clothed dip between her breasts, she shivered in anticipation.

His hand, resting lightly against the underside of her breast, began to move. Up, over, around, she arched with an ache she'd never known before. When he grazed her tight nipples with his thumb, she almost screamed.

"I'm never going to make it if we keep going like this," Nicole said, surprised at the huskiness in her voice.

Damien chuckled. "I want to enjoy this." He kissed the swell of her breast. "Every last minute of it."

He lowered her dress to bare a breast and took a nipple in his mouth. Nicole reached to pull him in tighter, begging him to take more of her. She tried to unbutton his shirt, but they were too close. She didn't want him to stop, but wanted to reciprocate.

He must have sensed her frustration, because he pulled back and edged off the bed. She took the hand he held out and stood. He turned her around and moved her hair over one shoulder. As he kissed her shoulder, she felt a tingle settle low in her back. When he moved to her neck and she felt the dress's zipper slide open from waist to buttocks, the shiver moved around to her belly to settle low.

The dress slid to the floor. Now she stood in nothing but a tiny pair of black underpants. A case of nerves set in again. This was the moment of truth. This is where she'd turn around and see. Either he liked her body or she'd catch that fleeting look of disappointment before he covered it up.

She turned slowly, taking a step back to put some space between them, staying focused on his eyes.

Eyes that held her gaze without wavering before drifting lower. And lower still until they reached her toes, then started a slow meandering rise back to her face. She watched him grin. Not like a man trying to seduce her, but like a boy in a candy store.

Nicole relaxed. He wanted her. She knew that now without a shadow of a doubt. When he reached for her, she stepped closer and nudged his arms to his sides.

One button at a time, she opened his shirt and then peeled it back. It joined her dress on the floor. Damien reached for her and she held him off. "You said you wanted to take it slow, right?"

He groaned. "Leisurely is one thing. You're going to kill me."

She ran both hands across his chest. She liked the smattering of dark chest hair. Not too much, just the perfect amount. Moving down his arms, he made it until she reached his hands and he grabbed for her.

"Uh uh. Not yet," she said laughing. She unbuckled his belt and tugged on it until it was free, tossing it over her back. The zipper of his slacks came next. When she started to slide them down, he grabbed her hands.

Lifting her, he settled her back in the middle of the bed, shrugged out of his slacks and joined her.

He then spent the next several minutes getting to know her body better, kiss by molten kiss. Always near, but never touching where she needed him to. When he finally dipped his hand beneath the lace, her body met him halfway and she begged for release.

"Not yet," he said, pulling back. "I want us to crash over the top together this first time.

"Then you'd better catch up."

He patted the lace, a finger slipping deep into the vee and it was Nicole's turn to gasp.

"I can't take much more." She kissed him and began her own exploration. She ran her fingers through the curls on his chest, well satisfied with the shudder that coursed through him. When she trailed her fingers down the line of hair on his abdomen, he held his breath.

"Breathe," she said with a wink. "You're going to need the oxygen."

He jerked as she feathered her fingers along his shaft. She watched, out of the corner of her eye, and a part of her wondered...he was so...

"We'll fit just fine," Damien whispered in her ear.

More than ready to find out, she grabbed him and he gasped. "I think," she said, "it's past time to test that theory."

"You are so right." He grabbed the ready condom and sheathed himself, raised over her, and paused with a look that said more than words to her. It seemed almost like...could he be looking at her with love in his eyes? Nicole shook her head.

"No?"

She smiled. "Not no. Yes. Yes, yes, yes."

He held her gaze as he entered her, taking his time, and she gasped as he filled her.

"Okay?"

"Very okay," she answered, then wrapped her legs around him as they moved in harmonized rhythm.

About the time she couldn't take it anymore, he groaned and moved faster. And faster. She matched his pace. And his desire.

In only moments, she felt the explosion of her climax as he let loose with his own. Even then, he didn't stop, keeping up slow, measured movements. She was surprised when the passion rose again, crashing into another crescendo of mind-numbing sensation.

He leaned on his elbows as they both gasped their way back to normal. When he rolled back to her side, Nicole approved wholeheartedly as he pulled her into his arms. She played with the hair on his chest as it rose and fell, his lungs still searching for a normal rhythm. Her own breathing struggled along with his.

Minute after minute, their bodies came down from the high of making love and drowsiness replaced wonder in Nicole's brain.

"That was amazing, Doctor," Damien said.

"Please," she said as her hand slowed its motion on his chest. "Call me Nicole."

His chuckle was the last thing she remembered as she drifted off to sleep.

"Nicole?"

"Mmmmmm." The voice filtered in, but didn't make sense. She'd been having the loveliest dream and longed to return to it. She'd been wrapped in Damien Reed's arms as they made slow, languorous love. Even in her sleep she knew turned on when she felt it.

"Come on, sleepyhead," the voice said again. "Time to wake up."

Funny. It sounded like Damien, but it couldn't be. He was still in her dream. Then fingers caressed her cheek and she remembered—everything. As a lazy smile spread across her face, she opened her eyes to the grinning face of her lover. And the man she would now, and for always, be over-the-top in love with.

"Welcome back to the land of the living," he said. "You don't wake up easily, do you?"

"Only when I'm having a dream I don't want to let go of."

He raised his eyebrows. "So, you were dreaming about me, were you?"

"Maybe. Maybe not."

"I think you were."

"Well, a woman's got to have some secrets." She stretched muscles still trying to wake up, raising her arms overhead to get maximum effect.

In doing so, the sheet that draped her slipped and Damien took advantage of the opportunity, kissing first one breast and then the other. "You have the most kissable breasts," he said.

Trying to think straight as need coursed through her, she shook her head. "They're too small."

"I disagree. From my vantage point, they are perfect." He cupped one in his hand and nuzzled it. "Absolutely perfect."

When he pulled a nipple into his mouth, Nicole decided to stop arguing with him. Except that moments later, he leaned away from her. She reached for him, but he shook his head. "I wish we had time. But we've slept longer than we should have already. We've got just enough time to shower and grab a bite to eat, after which we need to get on the road. It's Christmas Eve."

Her eyes widened. It *was* Christmas Eve. She hadn't even realized it. They needed to get on the road to his parents' house. She ran a hand lightly down his arm, wondering if maybe they should just stay here for Christmas. After all, he'd look pretty good in a big red bow—and nothing else.

"Don't even think about it," he said with a laugh.

"What?" She tried for a look of innocence.

"As much as I would love to spend Christmas in bed with you, my mother would kill us. Now go...you can have the shower first."

As she tumbled out of bed naked and headed for the bathroom, she glanced back, satisfied that he at least appeared regretful.

Moments later, steamy water calming her body, she was still having trouble putting their night's lovemaking into perspective.

She would meet his parents in just a few hours, and if she couldn't squelch the idea of dragging Damien back to bed, she'd ruin what was beginning to feel like a very important first meeting.

The shower curtain shifted and a naked Damien Reed stepped in. Nicole shrieked as he reached for her. "What are you doing? You said we didn't have time."

He shrugged. "I figure if we shower together, we're saving time, right?"

She cocked an eyebrow and felt passionate warmth fill her anew as he reached for the soap.

After a hurried breakfast and a call to his parents, Nicole and Damien got back on the road. The countryside sparkled with white, but at least it had stopped snowing. The plows had also been through, so with the road in better shape, they made good time.

As they turned down the drive to the home Damien had been raised in, Nicole gulped. The driveway was lined with snow-laden trees and seemed to go on for miles, like something out of the movies. Her nervousness increased with each tree they passed. Damien hadn't told her much about his home, or about his family. If the driveway was any indication, they lived in a mansion and he was filthy rich.

She gulped again. She'd never been around people who had a lot of money. She had no idea how to act.

Finally, they rounded one last corner and pulled up in front of a modest home. It was larger than anything she was used to, but surprisingly unassuming. A combination of brick and natural cedar shake siding, it looked built to meld with its surroundings instead of stand out. Along each window, a draping evergreen garland with small, white twinkling lights enhanced the effect of a warm, country home and Nicole sighed with happiness.

Damien opened her door and held his hand out. She took it and stepped out, glancing again at the house.

"Don't worry. My folks won't bite."

She smiled. "It's funny. A few minutes ago, I needed that reassurance. But this house…I don't know, it just feels…likes it's welcoming me."

He nodded with a smile of satisfaction. "I feel that way every time I come home."

Then the front door opened and a man and woman came out to greet them.

Nicole could not stop herself from staring at Damien's mother. Even with the gray starting to pepper in and the shorter style, the color was reminiscent of her own mother's hair. Plus she had a smile that felt as welcoming as her outspread arms. Damien Reed's mother wrapped those arms around Nicole and, for a moment, she was transported back in time. She was ten years old again and on the receiving end of her mother's hug.

Nicole returned the hug with a sense of happiness she hadn't felt for a long, long time. When she pulled away, she knew there were tears in her eyes and she didn't care.

It was hard to explain, but somehow, Nicole felt as if she'd just come home.

CHAPTER ELEVEN

Once inside, Damien helped Nicole off with her coat. As he hung it up, she took a moment to glance around. Christmas was everywhere. Every wall, table, doorway was decorated, yet it didn't overwhelm. It wasn't all lights and shiny objects. It was more wreaths and evergreen, muted ribbons, and other country décor.

The ambiance had a welcoming feel to it and Nicole embraced it. She wandered around the large living room and ran her hands along the garland adorning the fireplace. Damien's mother even had stockings hung. Seven of them. They had that amazing hand-quilted look to them. She smiled at the one with "baby to be" safety pinned to it. She fingered the one with Damien's name on it. It looked old, like it had maybe been his from childhood.

Next to it, a much newer one hung with the name Nicole stitched on it. She ran her hands along it as Damien wrapped his arms around her.

"Mom insisted. She called me to make sure she had the spelling of your name right and sewed it just this week."

Nicole tried very hard to keep the wobble out of her voice, but didn't quite succeed. "It was very sweet of her." Turning into his arms, she buried her face in his chest to hide the sheen of tears.

"Ahem."

Nicole jumped at the voice and tried to pull away. Damien only laughed and held on tighter.

"I'm not interrupting anything, am I?" The twinkle in his father's eyes set Nicole's mind to rest. Separating herself, she looked at Damien. "I need to thank your mother."

He nodded his approval as his father responded. "She's most likely in her favorite room in the house—the kitchen." He crooked a finger to show her the direction, but she didn't need it. She could follow the wonderful smells.

"Mrs. Reed?"

"In here," she called.

Nicole rounded the corner and stopped in her tracks. Where every other room was low key, comfortable, and country, the kitchen was huge and modern. Stainless steel appliances and granite counters gave way to the only country accent in the room—hickory cabinets.

"Wow," she said.

Grace Reed laughed. "You like it?"

"It's beautiful."

"And very functional. This was the one room I didn't care if it conformed to the rest of the house. My husband would like me to hire some help, but I love to cook," she said as she waved a hand around. "And this is my therapy room."

Nicole's eyes shone. "My grandmother would have loved this. She was always baking."

Grace patted one of the stools that bordered the central island in the kitchen. Nicole sat down as Grace ladled a cup of steaming liquid from a pot on the stove.

"Spiced cider. My own recipe," she said.

"Mmmm," Nicole said as she let the cup warm her hands and sniffed. "It smells wonderful. Thank you."

As Damien's mother went back to kneading what looked like bread dough, Nicole asked if she could help.

"Maybe later, dear. Right now, all I have left is to get this bread rising."

After some companionable silence, Damien's mother spoke up. "I understand your mother passed away when you were young?"

The question caught Nicole off guard and she felt her body clench in a knee-jerk reaction.

"I'm sorry. I shouldn't have asked," Grace Reed said.

"No. It's fine. I just...I don't know why I still react this way. It's been eighteen years since—" She gulped. "Since Mom passed away. I should be over it by now." She set the shaking cup of cider down before it spilled. Grace wiped her hands on a nearby towel and reached to cover Nicole's.

"You never get over it. And you shouldn't. You loved your mother and missing her is part of that, even after all these years."

"You—" Nicole cleared her throat and tried again. "You sound like you know."

"I do," Grace said. "I was a little older than you. My mother passed away when I was fifteen. I have learned to live with it. That doesn't mean I don't miss her to this day."

Nicole gripped Grace's hands and they stayed there for several long moments sharing private memories. When Grace pulled away to go back to her bread, she patted Nicole's hands.

Nicole spoke first. "I think she's the reason I love Christmas. It was her favorite holiday. She went overboard every year, to the point of bordering on corny." The memory cloaked her in warmth. "I always liked it."

"The good memories are the ones we treasure forever."

"Thank you," Nicole said. "I wish I had the words to explain how much I appreciate the stocking you made for me."

"You're welcome, dear. I want you to feel at home here."

"I do already."

"Good. Damien says you want to go into research?"

"Yes. Cancer research."

"Is that because of your mom?"

"Yes. She died from ovarian cancer."

"That's a nasty one. I had a good friend pass away a couple years ago from the same thing," Grace said.

Nicole took a sip of cider. "It is. And only nineteen percent are caught at stage one, where it's treatable. I'd like to increase those odds and find an early warning system."

"We certainly need it," Grace said, then paused. "I've only just met you, so feel free to tell me to go jump in the lake. But I need to ask. Won't you miss patient care?"

"No, I don't think so." Memories of those early weeks and how tough interaction with patients had been for her morphed into more comfortable moments. She'd never expected to like that end of things. It wouldn't sway her choice to go into research. But maybe she would miss it, just a bit.

"Damien says you have a knack for solving riddles."

Nicole smiled, pleased at the compliment.

"He also said you were very good with the patients."

Nicole chuckled. "He's stretching the truth with that one," she said.

"Stretching what truth?" Damien asked the question as he entered the kitchen. He sniffed the cider, reached for a cup and poured himself a ladleful, settling next to Nicole at the counter. Their knees touched and Nicole could feel the heat pass between them.

"You told your mother I was good with patients?"

"You are," he said without pause.

She looked at him, incredulous. "You've got to be kidding me. I'm a wreck with patients."

"You were at the beginning, but you got past it. You're great with them. Really." His brows knit together. "Don't you know that?"

She thought about it. It had gotten easier. In some cases, she'd found it quite easy to discuss symptoms and treatment with patients.

"Maybe," she said. "But I don't have your ability. You walk in a room and the patient feels better. You know patients and nurses alike call you Dr. Charisma behind your back, don't you?

"No!" He laughed. "And I believed I had my nose to the gossip scent. How did I miss that?"

Nicole laughed. "No one ever called you that outright? I'm amazed."

"Not even once," he said.

Nicole laughed when Damien shook his head, once again taken with the fact that the man did not fathom just how good-looking he was.

"It also," she continued, "helped you with the patients. That smile of yours disarms them when you enter the room."

Grace laughed. "We've always considered our son handsome, but it's nice to hear that from someone else."

Nicole glanced at Damien, and then turned for a second look. Did she really see a tinge of red creeping up his neck? Was the man actually embarrassed? That was a first, and she had to admit she liked it.

Damien cleared his throat. "Maybe this would be a good time to show you to your room," he said getting up.

His mother laughed. "Dinner will be in an hour, so don't be gone too long."

When she winked at Damien, Nicole felt the deep flush hit her cheeks. Could his parents know they'd spent the night together last night?

As she followed Damien upstairs, she wondered about the arrangements for their stay here. He wouldn't try to put them in the same room…in his parents' home. Would he?

He opened one of the doors off the hallway and she entered a room that was decidedly feminine. A white four-poster bed with eyelet lace was accented with blue and rose pillows. Posters of nineties rock stars adorned the walls and a corkboard over the chest of drawers was pegged with photos and award certificates.

Nicole looked closer. High school sports. Sarah Reed seemed to excel in the longer track events and in long jump.

She turned to Damien. "Sarah?"

"My baby sister," he said.

He'd mentioned a sister and brother-in-law. And the extra stocking in the living room meant she was pregnant.

"Sarah got married last year and they live about two miles away, so her room is pretty much the spare bedroom these days."

Nicole nodded. She cocked her head as she looked at Damien. "Any other family I should know about?"

He laughed. "No other siblings. A couple of aunts and uncles, none of which will be here for the holiday. Oh, but Sarah's pregnancy? She's very pregnant, as a matter of fact. I believe she's due in late January."

"With the first grandchild, I presume? Your mother must be thrilled."

"She is. And I'm indebted to my baby sister for taking the heat off me."

"To give your folks grandchildren?"

"Yes. I'd rather do it on my own timeline instead of to satisfy my mother's raging grandmother genes."

"She knows how gorgeous your children will be," Nicole said and then realized what she'd said. "I—I mean, when you have kids...I'm sure they'll be cute...sweet...you know, whenever you get married and have kids, that is."

Lame cover-up, Nicole. Really lame.

Damien reached for her but held her at arms length. "Hmmm," he said, giving her a critical once over. "Seems to me we'd make some pretty good-looking kids together."

Nicole felt the world slow its rotation. She could see the eyelet canopy swaying with air from the heat vent, but it moved in slow motion.

Damien kissed her. Not with the passion of last night, but with a sweeter, more endearing feeling. His lips moved over hers as if he cherished every touch. Already certain she loved Damien Reed, she knew now she would never love anyone else with the depth of emotion she felt for him.

Her arms traced the muscles of his back, reveling in the fact that, for however long this would last, she could touch him like this.

Reality returned in the form of a door crashing open downstairs and a very feminine "hello-o-o-o" reverberated throughout the house.

Damien let go of Nicole and she stood waiting for a wave of dizziness to abate. He turned to the window and muttered something about timing.

Nicole joined him and he put an arm around her shoulders as they watched Sarah and her husband unloading food dishes and gifts from the car.

"I need some distance from you or I'll never be able to go downstairs."

"What do you—oh!" The implications of what he said hit Nicole. "Ummm, all right. I could unpack?"

He nodded. "That would be good. I'll...unpack, too. Give me a few minutes and we'll go downstairs together."

Nicole smiled. "I'd like that."

He kissed her forehead and was out the door in a flash.

CHAPTER TWELVE

Nicole unpacked and wandered around the room, taking time to learn a little bit more about Sarah. She had to be close to Nicole's age, but what an overachiever. The diploma for her master's degree in education was framed on one wall and two class pictures filled with kindergarten children graced the wall beside it.

It was obvious Sara would make a great mother. Damien would be a good parent, too. This family seemed to foster that. Nicole wondered if she had the patience to raise children. She stood in front of the full-length mirror and swayed her back to round her stomach. She'd be a cute pregnant person. But could she raise a child? That took a lot of work.

And a lot of time. She frowned and straightened. She'd never imagined having kids. Her career had always been her goal and having children would change that. She touched one of the class pictures.

"I can't give up," she whispered. "I need to make a difference. I need to find a cure."

Laughter floated up from below just as she heard a knock on her door. "Ready?" Damien said.

"Uh, sure." she answered. She couldn't quite shake the feeling that she stood on the edge of some precipice. She tried. She shoved thoughts about babies to the back of her mind and planted a smile on her face as she turned.

"You okay?" Damien asked.

With a quick nod, she answered. "I'm fine." She widened her smile. "The real question is, are you?"

He took her hand. "As long as I don't get too close to you, I will be."

His comment wrapped her with a warm spirit that seemed completely in line with how this house, and this family, made her feel. It also did wonders to dispel the melancholy that had begun to settle on her shoulders.

They barely got through the kitchen door before a whirlwind threw herself at Damien. Sarah Reed-Campbell was a petite woman, dark-haired like her brother, but that was where the similarities ended. Where he was quiet and composed, she demanded attention just by entering a room.

"Damien!" she squealed as she continued to hug him. "I've missed you *so* much." She backed up and tapped his chest. "You need to come home more often, big brother."

No one escaped Sarah's attention, as she next wrapped her arms around Nicole. "It's so good to meet you. You're as gorgeous as my brother said. And I'm so glad you got him to come home for Christmas. He probably wouldn't have come if not for you. He's so wrapped up in his patients that he rarely leaves that hospital." Sarah nodded. "You, it seems, are a good influence on him."

Nicole barely kept up with Damien's fast-talking sister. Still, she learned some important tidbits of information from Sarah's one-way conversation, one of which was that Damien had told his sister she was beautiful. An unwarranted blush filled her cheeks at the second-hand compliment.

She also now knew he didn't come home often. She glanced at Damien and was surprised to see him squirming a bit under his sister's barrage. So the man had dodged a holiday or two because of work. His devotion to medicine rivaled her own single-mindedness. Nicole wondered how their respective careers would allow for raising a family. Maybe he didn't want children.

He placed a hand on his sister's bulging stomach. The animation on his face quickly put to rest the idea that he would not want kids.

Sarah still had not stopped talking.

"Sis, put a cork in it," Damien said. "Take a breath and give someone else a chance to talk."

Sarah stopped, but didn't look a bit sheepish.

Damien introduced Nicole to Sarah's husband, Mark, and the family went into dinner preparation mode, with Sarah giving orders and everyone following them.

"It's easier to just let her have her way," Damien whispered to Nicole.

"She's a powerhouse, isn't she?"

"She is that," he said, watching her hand the platter of prime rib to Mark.

"I like her. She's fresh and natural and makes folks smile."

"Definitely," he said. "Just don't tell her I said that."

"Said what?" Sarah came around the corner.

"That you're a brat," Damien countered.

"Of course I'm a brat. That's what little sisters are supposed to be, aren't they?"

Between Grace's talent in the kitchen and Sarah's organizational skills, they were soon seated at the dinner table with their plates laden with food. Conversation flew as they dished up. It felt like meals back home. Having grown up with a houseful of foster kids, noisy mealtimes were the norm for her. Nicole hadn't realized how much she'd missed it until now.

Was this what she wanted? A house full of family? Is this what Damien would want? She glanced at him as he bantered with his sister. Would he be willing to be with someone who wanted to wait to have children until she'd accomplished her career goals?

"Earth to Nicole," Damien whispered.

"Sorry," she said. "Day-dreaming, I guess."

He frowned. "You sure you're all right?"

No. I'm not. She and Damien had just started dating. It was too soon for her to be thinking about all this. She needed to let it go.

"Really. I'm fine," she said.

He gazed at her for another long moment before she saw his nod of acceptance.

Damien's father tapped his glass and stood as everyone quieted. "Christmas is a time of celebration on many different levels. Tomorrow, we celebrate Christ's birth. Tonight, we celebrate family. It's good to have all of you here. Our children—" He tipped his glass in turn to Damien and Sarah, then to Mark. "Our soon to be born granddaughter, and now Nicole, whom I feel certain we will see more of. Welcome to our family. Merry Christmas, everyone."

They all sipped their drink of choice. Nicole used the moment to try to get her emotions under control. She felt so welcomed by this family it was almost overwhelming.

Damien patted her knee under the table and she looked up at him and smiled as everything else faded away.

Later, they all dressed and went to midnight services, something Nicole had never done before. Her father and mother had always opted to go Christmas morning and then rush home for a big breakfast. It felt different, but not foreign. The church was decorated in trees and light. Sitting here felt calming and right. Having Damien's arm along the back of the pew offset that calmness and Nicole worked hard to concentrate on the services.

Afterwards, Sarah and Mark headed out with the promise that they'd be over in time for breakfast and gifts in the morning. Damien drove Nicole and his folks back to the house, where his parents retired almost immediately.

Damien poured a glass of wine for each of them and they settled on the couch to stare at the lights of the Christmas tree.

"How are you enjoying this Christmas?"

"Oh, Damien. I'm loving it." She turned to him. "You know my holiday looked rather bleak. You saw that and made it so much better than I could ever have imagined. Thank you for that."

"Then you're happy here?"

I'm at home here. "Yes. Your family has been great." She stared at the tree. She felt so welcomed, in fact, they had her re-thinking goals she'd held close to her heart since childhood.

Damien twirled a strand of her hair between his fingers. "I'm glad. I wanted you to like it here."

I like it so much, it's scary. "I do." She turned to him. "Something your sister said makes me think you don't come home every Christmas."

"I do come home for Christmas. They'd like me to come home more often."

"But your career is important to you."

He agreed. "There are always patients to treat. You know more than anyone how hard it can be to get away."

Damien didn't catch the hushed strain in her voice as he remained focused on her hair. "You probably don't want children when you marry, then. So you can focus on your patients."

"Not necessarily," he said, pulling a strand of hair to his nose and inhaling. "I think it's possible to have both."

"I don't see how," she mumbled, feeling the chasm widen between them.

He leaned in to nuzzle her neck. "I love how the pulse in your neck starts to race when I kiss you here. And here. And here."

Her body said enjoy, but her mind was racing and wouldn't stop. She pulled back. "You know how much going into cancer research means to me."

"Uh uh," he agreed, pulling her sweater back to gain access to her collarbone.

"I don't think I could have kids. At least not for quite a while. I'd need to reach my research goals, first."

She felt him pull back as it finally registered that this was something important to her. "You mean you want to find a cure for cancer before you can think of having children?"

"It's been my focus for years."

"Why can't you do both?" he asked. "I could have a medical practice and still raise a family. Why not you?"

"Because research means long hours."

"So we switch off duties between the long hours and the family stuff. Except at first, of course. I can't carry the baby, give birth, or recover for you."

"Exactly." She winced at the raised tone of her voice. "We can't even consider it until I'm further along in my work."

"That a bit ridiculous, don't you think?" He ran his hands through his hair. "Why are we even having this conversation, anyhow?"

"Because I see how good you are with kids. How much you enjoy even your sister's pregnancy. I don't know if I could give you that...give any man that."

"Why not?" His voice powered up to her level and Nicole stiffened.

"Nicole, is this really something we have to sort out now? This holiday is important. Why can't we simply enjoy it? We're friends, right?"

Her mouth went dry, all thoughts of procreation gone in an instant. After what they'd shared, he considered them only friends? "Friends?" She croaked the word out, afraid to try to say more.

"You know what I mean," he said.

She pushed him back and stood, waiting for the pain running through her heart like an electrical current to ebb. It didn't. "You see us as friends with benefits?"

"No. I think we're much more than that."

"So did I," she said.

"What's the matter?"

"Just so you know, Damien. I don't sleep around."

He shook his head and his eyes registered surprise. "I didn't think you did."

"Sleeping with you was more than just a 'friends with benefits' thing for me."

"It was for me, too."

"Well, that doesn't seem to be the case based on what's coming out of your mouth."

Now he looked really confused, but she didn't care. "I'm going to bed," she said and fled up the stairs.

In her bedroom, she collapsed onto the bed. What had she been thinking? That the man might actually love her?

She began to throw her clothes in her bag and then realized there were no taxis out here in the country. Pulling back the window shade, she saw it had started to snow again. How was she going to leave?

She slumped onto the bed and crumpled into the fetal position. Damien didn't love her. She should be happy about that. It ended her quandary. She could go on with her research goals and not worry about relationships and families and...and children.

She clutched her stomach. So why was she so miserable? Unable to find a way past a despair that made her heart hurt. And how would she endure spending Christmas Day with a man who did not return her love.

Changing into a nightgown her parents had sent her in an early Christmas package, she walked over and stared out at the snowy landscape. Had it only been a few hours ago it had seemed so cheerful and homey?

When she heard a soft tap at her door, she padded over and opened it. Damien stood there, still fully clothed. And looking decidedly haggard.

"Can I come in?"

"Why?"

"Please? I need to talk to you. And I can't do it out here."

"Why not?"

"Because my parents are sleeping across the hall, for one thing."

She didn't want to let him in, didn't want to have the conversation they needed to have. Yet some perverse side of her opened the door wider. She left him to close it and walked back over to the window. She turned, ready to beat him to the punch, but stopped short.

Damien had not moved from the closed door. He stood there with wide eyes and his mouth hanging open. That's when Nicole glanced down and saw how diaphanous her nightgown was, especially with snow-light streaming in through the window.

Let him look. Let him see what he'll be missing. She had the satisfaction of seeing his Adam's apple bob up and down. Damien reached for a throw blanket and held it out to her.

"I think you'd better put this on so I can have a clear head. Apparently, being aroused by your nearness muddles mine and I say the wrong thing."

She wrapped the blanket around her and went to sit in the window seat. When Damien settled across from her, she tucked her feet up under her. Touching him would be too much to bear.

"I said the wrong thing earlier."

Nicole started at him.

"You know, downstairs? By the tree?"

"Yes. I know."

He laid a hand on her knee, but she stiffened so he pulled it back. "I'm sorry."

Nicole shook her head and sighed. In her heart, she knew he was sorry he couldn't return her love. And she didn't have the heart to make him suffer because of it. "I know you are."

His smile was tentative. "Good. I don't want us to fight. I want this Christmas to be special."

This Christmas would definitely stand out as the most memorable one she'd ever had. Nicole wished the deep ache in her chest would go away. It was too hard to be close to him and not be with him.

Then he smiled and her heart broke in two. "It's only a few short hours until morning and we both need some sleep." He stood and kissed the top of her head. "Thanks, honey. I don't want you upset, and I'd like us both to enjoy tomorrow."

After he closed the door behind him, Nicole laid her head in her arms and let the tears flow. Tomorrow would be the hardest day of her life.

CHAPTER THIRTEEN

A few sleepless hours later, Nicole heard motion in the hall as someone made their way downstairs. She got up and stared into the mirror at bleary, tear-streaked eyes, wondering how she'd ever make herself presentable.

After a long shower, she dressed in her favorite holiday skirt and sweater, applied some makeup, and prayed it would hide her all but sleepless night. Pleased with how well her efforts worked, she squared her shoulders and prepared to endure what would probably be the longest Christmas Day of her life.

She took the gifts she'd brought down to place them under the tree. It wasn't much. Seattle coffee for the Reeds and a little something for Damien. Following the smell of brewed coffee to the kitchen, Nicole found Damien's mother dressed and quietly preparing breakfast.

"Merry Christmas," Grace said, stopping long enough to hug Nicole.

Tears stung her eyes, but she willed them away and hugged the woman back. When they separated, Grace gave Nicole a long look. "Did you sleep well?"

Nicole shrugged. "Well enough."

"Is everything all right?" Worry was evident in her voice.

Nicole put on what little of a poker face she had and reassured Damien's mother that all was well.

"Good." She patted Nicole's cheek. "There should be no sadness on Christmas."

Nicole nodded, afraid her voice would break if she agreed out loud. "Can I help?" She waved at the counter.

"Definitely," Grace said, handing her an apron. "Why don't you finish up the bacon and sausage? I've already got the ham cooked and potatoes in the oven. I just need to finish the eggs. By then, Sarah and Mark will be here."

They had just about finished preparations when Damien and his father walked in. His dad went straight for the coffee pot, while Damien went first to Nicole and leaned down to kiss her cheek in greeting.

If she stiffened a little, it was just to help remember to keep her distance. When he frowned, she knew he'd felt it. Too bad. He'd have to get used to some boundaries.

Damien poured a cup of coffee and took a slow sip.

They all turned at the sound of the front door. "Merry Christmas," Sarah called, rushing into the kitchen.

"Mark's putting the last of our presents under the tree. I promised I'd bring him coffee." She poured a cup, started to walk out of the kitchen, then turned back to them. "Come on…let's go unwrap gifts!"

Grace laughed. "We should eat breakfast first."

"Aw, come on, Mom. You say that every year."

"And every year you talk me out of it."

"Then it's settled. We open gifts first. Besides," she continued, her hands enfolding her stomach. "You're not going to make your grandchild wait until after breakfast, are you?"

Even Nicole had to laugh at the lopsided logic Sarah used. Still, everyone grabbed their cups and followed her to the living room. Nicole sat in one of the overstuffed chairs, thinking Damien would not be able to sit next to her that way, but he thwarted her plan and perched on the arm of the chair. With his hand resting on the high back of the chair, she couldn't move without touching him in some way or another. And every touch singed her heart even further.

"So, who gets to go first?" Sarah asked, wagging her eyebrows at her brother, who groaned.

"You are horrible at keeping secrets, sister."

"Well, if you'd get on with it, there wouldn't be any more secrets to keep."

With a disgusted sigh, Damien set down his coffee cup and stood up.

"So I get to hand out the first gift?"

He looked at each member of his family and waited as they nodded their heads. Nicole was confused. It was as if they knew something she wasn't privy to.

Damien reached behind the tree and pulled out a small box, holding it behind his back as he turned to Nicole. "I considered doing this in private," he said.

She frowned. Doing *what* in private.

"But family is important to you, right?"

She nodded, glancing at the eager faces of his parents and his sister, still not comprehending what was going on.

"I know that Christmas carries strong memories of your mother," he said.

Nicole jerked her head back around to stare at him. Why was he talking about her mother?

"I hoped this might be a way that her memory could share this moment with us."

When he went down on one knee and held out the jeweler's box out, Nicole's heart skipped about three beats before hitting the wall of her chest and breaking through.

"Nicole Milbourne, I've been in love with you since I first walked into that patient's room and you bobbled the swab kit you were holding. Earlier, if I were truthful. At orientation it took everything I had to keep from asking you out right then and there."

She gulped, not able to fully wrap her mind around what he was saying. Hadn't he called them friends with benefits last night? No, that had been her. Had she misinterpreted his words?

"I would have preferred to meet your parents before asking you this," he continued.

Was this really happening?

"But I did speak to your father on the phone before they left on their cruise."

"You spoke to my f-father?" she asked. "When?"

"I called him the day before they left."

"You've—you've been planning this for that long?"

"Longer. And, in case you're interested, your father gave me his blessing."

He leaned in to whisper in her ear. "Don't worry about the kids thing. We work well together. We'll figure it out."

She could feel tears sting her eyes as her heart thudded inside her chest. When he reached for her hand and placed it against his own chest, she felt his heart racing along with hers.

"I can't imagine a life without you. Will you consent to marry me, Nicole Milbourne? Will you spend the rest of your life with me as I want to spend the rest of mine with you?"

"I-I thought you only wanted to be friends." She still couldn't quite wrap her head around the idea.

He glanced at his parents, then lowered his voice. "I never wanted to be just friends." The gleam in his eyes validated what he said.

Nicole's heart filled with the love she was now free to feel and to show. She could feel his heartbeat beneath her hand. She poured all the love she felt for him into her voice.

"My heart matches yours beat for beat. It always has...and always will. I love you."

"And?"

"Yes," she said. Then again, she whispered. "Definitely yes."

"Halleluia!" He pulled her up and swung her around in circles. When her feet found ground again, his family surrounded them with hugs and congratulations.

"Well," Sarah said after things settled down. "I doubt anything will outdo that gift, but how about we open the rest of these wonderful boxes."

Nicole settled back into the chair, this time more than happy to have Damien sitting beside her. His arm along the back of the chair now comforted her. His other hand only left hers long enough to open a gift or allow her to open one.

When he handed her another gift, it surprised her.

"A ring at Christmas should stand alone," he said. "That wasn't your gift, it was mine."

She glowed. "It was the only gift I need."

"Go, ahead," he said, pride evident in his voice. "Open it."

She unwrapped a frame. It was a majestic photo of Mt. Rainier. She touched the frame, nostalgia washing over her. This wasn't just any picture of the mountain. The meadow in the forefront was in high spring and alive with the purples and yellows of wildflowers, with the mountain in the background holding on to the white of winter.

It would always remind her of home. She raised eyes filled with love to Damien. "Thank you," she said.

He leaned down for a kiss. "You're welcome. But that's not all. Turn it over.

She did so, and found an envelope on the back. Opening it, she saw a receipt for a significant donation to the American Cancer Society...in memory of Celia Milbourne.

Her mother.

She clutched the paper. "It's too much," she whispered to Damien.

"We all chipped in." Damien waved his arm at his smiling, nodding family.

"I'm...humbled. Thank you so much."

Grace rose and set a hand on Nicole's shoulder. "We know how much your mother meant to you. And that you've had a happy life with your father and step-mother. Now, you have more family. And, hopefully, another mother to love."

Nicole stood and gave Grace a hug that was tight and heart-felt, at a complete loss for words.

After that, the gift opening hit high gear. When Nicole handed a package to Damien. "It's not much." She glanced at the ring adorning the third finger of her left hand. "Certainly nothing as precious as what you've given me."

He opened it and found a photo album, hand-decorated with the words "Dr. Damien's kids". He looked at her and she could tell he didn't get it.

"You still intend to go into general practice, right?"

"Yes. I believe it's where I'll be most useful."

She touched the book. "It's for all the babies you'll help bring into the world."

He spread his hand over the book and smiled. "I like that idea." He looked at Nicole. "I like it a lot, actually."

She blushed as the meaning of his words sank in, then slapped his arm. "First things first. You may be graduated, but I still have a residency program to get through."

"True." Damien covered her hand with his. "You're going to be a great researcher."

"Yes," she nodded. "I am."

"And, when you're ready," he whispered, "we'll talk about kids. Okay?"

Breakfast that morning rivaled any holiday memory Nicole held in her heart. When Grace and Sarah shooed her away from dish duty, she wandered into the living room and stared at the Christmas tree. She reached out to touch a crystal angel hanging from one of the limbs, feeling more than ever that her mother was here with her today. Here celebrating in the season. Here to witness the birth of a new family.

Damien's arms circle her waist and he pulled her into his chest. "Happy?"

"Oh, yes. More than ever."

"Me, too." They stood there, quietly staring at the tree for some time. "I wish I'd known your mother," Damien said into her ear.

"I wish you had, too." Nicole turned in his embrace. "You kind of do, though. There are a lot of similarities between your mother and mine."

"Then I know I would have loved her."

She twined her arms around his neck. "She'd have loved you, too. You know, I always believed she was what was missing in my life."

"Having a mother?"

"Not necessarily. Kate did a great job of raising me. I know that. But I always had to share that love with all the foster kids she cared for. I thought...I thought that if I could just go back to the small family I started out with. Just me and my mom...that I'd know again the safety and joy of true family."

"And now?"

Nicole smiled up at him. "Now I understand better. It's not the size of the family. It's the love you give to it and that it gives back to you. I had that with Kate and Dad. I was so focused on the memory of my mother, I didn't recognize what I had." She frowned. "I did Kate a disservice. I've never called her 'Mom' and that's exactly what she's been to me all these years. I just refused to accept it."

"When I spoke to your father, she was also on the phone. Her happiness for you, for us, was very apparent. Kate loves you very much."

Nicole snuggled into Damien's embrace, feeling the last pieces of her life puzzle fall into place. "You know, I think we will make beautiful children."

He laughed and squeezed her tight. "When we're both ready, we definitely will."

"I love you so much it scares me," she whispered into his chest.

"I know what you mean," he answered, his breath rustling her hair as he spoke. "I've never felt this way before."

He tipped her head up and lowered his face to hers. "We'll figure our way through it all together."

"I like that idea."

He kissed her then, a kiss filled with gentle promise. Nicole felt forever in his touch and returned it with all her heart and soul.

EPILOGUE

Nicole watched the flurry of activity around her. It seemed silly to make this much fuss, but here they were. Her mother was trying to get Hailey's dress over her head and the three-year old simply would not cooperate.

Shaking her head, Nicole remembered the aftermath of that Christmas three years ago. Her father and stepmother had stopped over on their way home to congratulate her on the engagement...and to officially meet her fiancé. They'd brought their own news. Fate drove them right by an orphanage and, upon visiting, they'd fallen deeply in love with then six-month old, auburn-haired Hailey. Nicole now had a little sister.

Damien's mother was zipping the dress of a very pregnant Sarah, who kept a careful eye on her already dressed three-year old son. Mark, Jr. and Hailey had been inseparable since her family's arrival two days ago. Inseparable...and holy terrors. Nicole sent a prayer to heaven that twins did not run on either side of the family.

Everyone bustled around and she almost laughed at the chaos. All for a single moment in time. It seemed so silly. Today didn't matter. The fact that she and Damien had the rest of their lives together, that was what mattered.

And that attitude had gotten her into trouble more times than she could count over the past several months. With her Mom. With Grace. And with Sarah.

She figured if it was so important to them, let them plan it. But they would have none of it. They'd gotten together behind her back and schemed to involve her, spiriting her away on girls' weekends here and there to shop for dresses, to check out caterers, and to look at cakes. The type of planning that wasn't easy to achieve when they lived on separate coasts.

So here she sat, professional makeup starting to itch on her face. She'd drawn the line at a hairstylist, preferring to leave her hair down in simple curls, just the way Damien liked it. Of course, it would be hidden by the veil they'd talked her into, but at least that was a simple piece that hung from a small banded tiara.

She picked at a piece of fuzz on the white sweats she wore, a gift at the surprise wedding shower they'd thrown her two nights ago. She'd been vehemently opposed to any parties. The women in this family didn't quite seem to understand that she just wanted to be married to Damien.

Very soon now she would get to walk down that aisle with a church full of peoples' eyes centered on her and her alone. She could feel the sweat forming on her skin. Wondering again why they hadn't eloped, she saw her mom shooing everyone out of the room.

"It's time, honey. Let's get you dressed," she said.

Nicole stood, the feeling of being led to the guillotine strong. Did all brides get this nervous about their wedding day? For these same reasons?

She stripped off the sweats praying this day would be speed by. Slipping her arms through the skirt and into the sleeves, the soft whoosh of the satin as it settled over her had a strange calming effect.

She'd chosen an all-satin strapless dress that had a lace overlay with long sleeves. Nicole stood patiently as her mother buttoned up the dress.

When she turned, Kate had tears in her eyes. "You are such a beautiful bride, Nikki."

"Thank you, but you're my mother. You're prejudiced."

Her mom shook her head, turning Nicole toward the mirror. "Look for yourself."

Nicole stared at the image that looked back at her. The white...they'd talked her out of ivory...really did make her skin color glow in contrast. The makeup was artfully deceptive.

Her eyes looked larger, her cheeks more prominent, and her lips perfectly shaped. Yet it all looked very natural.

Even the veil framed her auburn hair and made it appear effervescent.

Nicole felt like a princess going to her first ever ball. She turned to see Kate with a wistful smile and tears in her eyes.

"Your mother would have loved to see how beautiful you are right now," Kate said, giving Nicole a careful hug.

It was Nicole's turn to go misty. She set her hand on Kate's arm. "I'm sorry."

"For what?"

"If I ever made you feel you weren't my mother. You were, you know. You taught me what I needed to know to get to this day. You stepped into," Nicole gulped, "some big shoes without complaint. And all I ever did was give you flack for it."

"Is that what you think?"

Nicole nodded.

"Honey, I knew the relationship you had with your mother was a very rare and precious one. I never felt slighted or second best. Our relationship was different, and that's how it should be. I always believed you loved me. And I've always loved you."

"I do love you, Mom." Hugging again, they both dabbed at their makeup and made a pact—no more crying today.

A soft knock on the door heralded company. Kate went to answer it, then slipped out as Nicole's father stepped inside. And stopped short, his mouth gaping open.

Nicole smiled as she watched him take two big gulps of air. He gulped a third time before he found his voice. "I can't believe this is my little Nikki," he said, his voice breaking.

"I'm the same little girl, Daddy."

"No. I don't think you'll ever be the same again. But that little girl who loves to make everything right, she's inside you." He took both her hands. "I'm more proud of you than I can say, sweetheart." Spreading her arms, he continued. "I can't believe my baby's about to get married."

Nicole nodded through the sheen in her eyes.

"And a fully accredited doctor to boot. Dr. Nicole Milbourne."

She shook her head. "Soon to be Dr. Nicole Milbourne-Reed."

Her father smiled. "I like that you kept your mother's name."

"Me, too. It's kind of like she's here, you know?" Nicole swallowed. "Like she's still a part of my life?"

"She always will be, Babydoll. She always will be."

The strains of music selected as a prelude to her entrance wafted through to them just as the wedding coordinator opened the door. "It's time."

Nicole walked out on her father's arm and watched as the wedding party moved into the church two by two. Finally, it was her turn to move into place. She gazed in awe at the yards of tulle, twinkling lights, and the church filled with people. It looked like a fairytale.

Maybe this formal wedding thing wasn't such a bad thing after all.

And at the front of it all, standing tall and handsome in his black tuxedo, stood the reason for all of it.

Damien Reed. Her love. Her friend. Her life.

Nicole glanced up at the rafters. "See Mom. I'm going to be just fine." A ray of winter sunshine filtered through, as if in happy response.

Then the music changed and Nicole stepped forward into her new life.

Author's Note: Nicole's goals in life changed when she was nine years old and her mother was diagnosed with stage three ovarian cancer. If you'd like to read Celia Milbourne's heartfelt journey and see how nine-year-old Nikki handles all the ups and downs of her mother's treatment, is now available at most major etailers. For more information, please consider joining my .

BOOKS BY LAURIE RYAN

Contemporary Romance stories

<u>Billionaire Bachelor Pledge series</u>

Royal Flush

High Card

All In

Full House

Blind Bet

<u>Willow Bay series</u>

Last Resort

Finding Home

Chances Are

Tender Tide

Reluctant Christmas

Operation Ethan

<u>Tropical Persuasions series</u>

Stolen Treasures

Pirate's Promise

Dare to Love

<u>Standalone</u>

The Long Journey Home

Rudy's Heart

Lost and Found

Northern Lights

Healing Love

<u>Women's Fiction</u>

Show Me

<u>Fantasy</u>

Survival

Enlightenment

Birthright

Awakening

Wolf's Call

About the Author

Laurie Ryan writes about resilient, independent women who might stumble, but they dust themselves off and get the job done. Their men, whether commanding alpha or endearing cinnamon roll heroes, will do whatever it takes to ensure the happiness of the women they cherish.

Laurie lives in the Pacific Northwest with her "he can fix anything" hubby, but is always willing to travel to visit their children and grandchildren. Her creativity isn't limited to writing. She also scrap books and, when she really needs to disappear, she paints rocks and shells found on the beaches she walks at the ocean—her happy place.

Laurie has always had a deep connection to nature and the outdoors, which is reflected in her writing. She is a passionate writer who brings her love for nature, animals, and creativity into her work.

An avid cruiser, Laurie has visited many places. One of her favorites was a stop in Greenland, where the strength and endurance of the people living in those beautiful but harsh surroundings became an underlying thread in her stories. Her sensual romance novels are sure to warm the hearts of readers.

Connect with Laurie on Facebook, Instagram, or TikTok, or her website, and join Laurie's newsletter for up to date news and releases.

Laurie loves to hear from her readers and can be reached at laurie@laurieryanauthor.com

SNEAK PREVIEW

RUDY'S HEART

By Laurie Ryan

The Story

An uncle-turned-father, terrified he'll screw up, enlists the help of a burned-out, empathic woman with an oh-so-rightful chip on her shoulder.

Emotionally shattered from her hospice work, Aubrey Gannet journeys to a Montana ranch looking for peace and quiet to rekindle her grieving spirit. But will she be able to forgive the man who deserted his only sister when she needed him the most?

Stuck with an angry horse no one can get near and a child

who refuses to speak, loner Beck Hawthorne is desperate to get through to them and hoping Aubrey Gannet holds that key. Only together can they break the bonds of sadness and find a brighter future.

Emotional. Sensual. Standalone. A romance novel that includes a wonderfully intuitive horse named Rudy and a six-year-old who will wrap herself around your heart. #contemporaryromance #horseranch #montana

SNEAK PEEK

Chapter One

Tail flying high, the horse raced to the far end of the corral and reared when the fence prevented his escape. He whirled around, kicking at fence boards that bounced with the force of the blow but withstood the battering. Once, twice, three times he kicked. When he finally dropped to four legs, he stood there shivering, his coat glossy with sweat.

Beck Hawthorne settled a booted foot on the lowest board and leaned on the fence, wondering for the thousandth time in the last month why he'd taken on this horse. Brought to Beck from an abusive situation, Rudy wouldn't let a soul near him. He'd bitten two of Beck's men and tried to kick a third when they'd moved him from the trailer to this corral. When they'd tried to bathe him, he'd fought until they were forced to stop or risk injury, to the horse or to them. Rudy had been so terrified, Beck couldn't put him through that again. Now, Beck wouldn't let any of his men near the horse. He alone set out food and mucked out the lean-to at the end of the corral, the one they'd built so Rudy would have more shade and a place to eat. Not that he'd gotten any thanks for it. Nope. Nothing but angry puffs of air from the far side of the corral whenever he entered with food or pitchfork. Rudy ate the feed, but only after Beck retreated from sight.

How could he get through to this animal? Everything he'd tried so far had dismal results. And now his young niece seemed taken with the horse. Damn it. Beck slapped the fence and the horse jumped even with the distance between them. He yanked his hat off and wiped sweat from his brow with his arm.

"Beck?"

Cassidy, the face of Hope Ranch and Beck's go-to for all things organizational, stood several feet back, toying with a strand of kinky hair that had four or five colors woven through it, colors that complemented her dark skin. She eyed the horse as she held out a phone. "Mara's asking for you and won't take no for an answer."

Mara. His favorite cousin, even if she was a royal pain in the ass. Okay, his only cousin. With a last glance at the horse, Beck thanked Cassidy and took the phone.

"Hey, Mars."

"Yeah, and that nickname never gets old," she drawled. "How's my favorite little girl doing?"

Dani. The niece he'd been given sole custody of. The worry knot in Beck's throat tightened. "She's no better, no worse. She's healthy, fed, seems content. I just can't get her to open up, to tell me how to help her."

"Give it time," Mara said. "It hasn't been that long."

"It's been months."

"Not very many, though. Grief takes its own time. She'll let you know when she's ready to talk. In the meantime, just love her and let her enjoy the ranch. By the way, where the heck were you hiding? I could have painted my nails and dried them in the time it took your assistant to find you."

"I live on a ranch now, remember? Nothing's a short walk. You know that." He nodded to Cassidy, thinking that would act as a dismissal, but she stayed where she was. Beck should have known better. His ranch manager's daughter kept this place running smoothly, though her attitude got a bit proprietary at times.

"Yes, dear cousin, I do," Mara said. "Speaking of which, how's everything going?"

Beck headed back toward the house. When Cassidy fell in step beside him, he glared at her, but he knew she wouldn't budge. If she wasn't so good at her job ...

"Things are slow," he told Mara. She had a right to know. She'd been there to help for the first couple weeks after he'd bought the place. "The barn is ready and I'm searching for the right quarter horses to begin the breeding program. Since it could take years for that to be profitable, I hope to bring in several hundred head of cattle this fall, which means we're working on fencing."

"And the house?"

"The bed and breakfast is a low priority, but it's coming along."

"Good, because I've got your first customer, a woman I know."

"Mars, we're not open yet." The B&B idea had been Cassidy's. Beck had thought her nuts, but anything that would make some money for the pit into which he'd sunk a huge chunk of his finances couldn't be a bad idea, right? Now, he was back to thinking it was crazy.

"It will be a good run-through for the guest part of your ranch. And she'll be no trouble. She just needs a place to rest for a while."

Rest? How old was this woman? "Absolutely not. I don't even have the rooms furnished yet. The furniture doesn't arrive for another two weeks."

"Then move a bed, dresser, and chair from the bunkhouse to that room at the front. It's the quietest and has the best view."

Instantly, Beck regretted Mara's visit to the ranch after his niece came to live with him. She'd been a huge help, but the woman remembered too much.

"Come on, Beckett. She needs a break and you need a test guest. It's a win-win."

The sting of hearing that name punched Beck in the gut. He hadn't gone by that in years. Since college, to be exact. Since his father, Beckett, Sr., had died, along with Beck's mother. Beckett brought back too many memories, some of which were tied to fresh wounds.

"We could bring furniture up, but— "

"Good, because her name is Aubrey Gannet and she's already on her way."

"What?"

"Yep. I saw her off this morning. Figured you'd come around and recognize the benefit for both of you. She's driving from Seattle and isn't a speedy traveler, so it'll be three days before she arrives. She won't stay long. I promise. Just a few days."

Great. Some old woman who drove fifty miles per hour on the freeway. Beck pictured her on Montana's highways, a line of traffic honking behind her. "That's not enough time," he told Mara.

"Sure it is. But Becky?"

And there it was. The other name he preferred to never hear again. He hated that childhood name, gifted to him by the one and only Mara. If she weren't the one person he could count on, he'd give her an earful.

"Take it easy on her, okay? She's had it rough and really needs to rest."

"Who are you sending me? Someone who's sick or something?"

"Not sick. Tired."

Great. Not only a guest he wasn't ready for, but a guest with issues. Beck glanced back at Rudy, who'd moved to his fresh food. In the opposite direction, Dani stared through a window, another lost soul, her eyes riveted on that damn horse. The look of longing on her face was something Beck didn't need words to decipher. Grief had turned his six-year-old niece into a silent ball of sadness. She seemed lonely, too, though she was rarely alone. Now, some old lady who'd probably need more help than Mara thought was on her way to join them. From Seattle. Where Dani had lived until coming to live with him.

Somehow, he'd become a home for wounded souls. Beck clicked off the call with Mara and handed the phone to Cassidy, who'd kept pace with him.

"It seems we're about to have company. Have someone bring up the best bed and dresser from the bunkhouse and put it in the front bedroom upstairs."

"Who's coming?"

"I have no idea. Mara sent her. Some lady who needs to rest. Apparently, we've turned into a recovery home for the aged. And the young. And horses."

~~~

"What have you gotten me into?" Aubrey Gannet muttered, and not for the first time, to the woman listening on the other end of the phone, the culprit behind her predicament.

"This will be good for you," Mara said. "You need to get away for a while."

"I need to relax, not disappear. I just left Butte, and it already seems like I'm in the middle of nowhere." She'd left her comfort zone way behind. It had been a while since she'd traveled anywhere except to visit patients, and now, she was two states away from home and lost. It had taken her until well past noon to find the motivation to get going, which left zero time to un-lose herself. "Plus, didn't you say it would be temperate this time of year?"

A sheen of sweat covered the tops of her hands and her palms stuck to the steering wheel. Aubrey peeled them off and wiped them, one at a time, on her jeans. Sweat was her nervous release, though it generally made matters worse rather
~~~

than better. Still, today was sweltering. Her old car overheated without much convincing. Not wanting to break down on the far side of nowhere, she'd opted for windows-down air conditioning, though that resulted in the scent of sun-baked everything permeating the air inside her car.

"If there's nothing around you, you must be close, which means you're going to lose cell service soon."

"Lose cell service?" Oh, this was so going from bad to worse.

"Yes … remember … relax and don't … anyone ask you … help. Tell … him … be nice. Goodb— "

With that unfinished word, Aubrey's cell cut out, apparently for the duration of her visit to Nowhere, Montana.

Running a hand along her neck, Aubrey yanked her ponytail, a miserable failure at keeping her cooler, over her shoulder. She sighed. How had Mara talked her into this? A week ago, she'd shown up at Aubrey's apartment with a bottle of wine. By the end of that bottle, she'd elicited a promise from Aubrey—a mandatory vacation—and had held her to it. Her friend had taken total advantage of her moment of weakness.

Aubrey needed a break. She knew that. Too much death had visited her of late. Normally, she handled that a lot better. As a hospice social worker, she considered it an extraordinary privilege to help patients cross that final threshold in as peace-filled a way as possible. That never used to get to her. Hope's passing had broken her, though. Work, life, everything – it all seemed so futile.

Hope Jones, the dark-haired, thirty-one-year-old with brown, soulful eyes, had handled her cancer with quiet calmness, her entire focus on her young daughter. Seeing that relationship, Aubrey had longed for her own family, her own children.

Then Hope died and the little girl drew into herself. Nothing Aubrey did brought the girl out of her shell. She'd tried over several days to help the silent sadness in the six-year-old's face, to no avail. Aubrey had considered trying to fast-track a foster-parent application.

That's when the child had disappeared. Whisked away by some relative Hope had only mentioned once, and even then, she'd barely said anything. A brother. He'd never come to visit Hope in the months Aubrey had been part of her life. And Hope's no-account ex-husband had disappeared before the positive symbol on the pregnancy test had become clear. Hope had confided in Aubrey that the man had sent papers giving up all his rights to his daughter in the same envelope as the divorce papers.

Had Hope asked her no-account brother to take the child? Aubrey had a hard time believing she would do that. Aubrey had tried to find the six-year-old. No matter how much Aubrey begged child services, no one would tell her where the brother lived. Even Mara, the girl's cousin, had been close-mouthed, giving Aubrey some cockamamie story that she needed to heal herself first.

After that, her job became more burden than blessing. She'd tried to give her patients the best care, to hide her tears for the families and friends. She'd buried her own emotions pretty well, she'd thought. Until her boss put her on a mandatory leave of absence.

"Get your head back in the game and your heart out of it." Gwen said the words with gentle effect, and then reminded Aubrey how good she was at hospice work and that they'd hate to lose her.

"Burnout is real," Gwen said.

So, after two weeks of Aubrey barely sleeping and eating, Mara had shown up at her door.

Aubrey glared at the semi-arid, empty landscape passing by her car window. Friend or no friend, when she got home, she would pound Mara.

After another mile, fenced fields appeared on both sides of the road. Then, finally, the typical tall wooden and metal structure that heralded the entrance to a ranch. Aubrey turned off the road and stopped. A mailbox had the name Hawthorne on it. That's the name Mara had given her. Her gaze moved up to the sign swaying in the welcome breeze.

Hope Ranch.

Aubrey's heart pounded, her hand the only thing keeping it from thumping right out of her chest. The name brought all the pain and grief, never far from her mind, roaring to the forefront. She looked at the address Mara gave her. The same numbers were screwed to the fence post in front of her. This was the right place.

Had Mara known? Aubrey swiped at the tears that fell unbidden. Hope. Too young to have her life snuffed out. The pain was real. Her gut spasmed as she thought of the last moments in her friend's life. And now the grief surged, being here, at a place with her friend's name on the front gate. She got out of the car and walked to the fence, looking each way at the long stretch of board and post that followed the road until she couldn't see it anymore. Her hand hovered over the wood for a long moment before resting on its roughness.

Hope.

I miss you so much.

How had Mara found this place? Sent her here? Aubrey couldn't do this. Couldn't stay where everything would be wrapped around memories of her lost friend. She got in her car, resolute about turning around, heading back to Butte. Grabbing the steering wheel, she leaned forward and rested her forehead on her hands.

It hurt so much. Everything hurt. How was she ever going to be happy again?

She gazed up at the stylized sign, remembering how Hope had whiled away hours with pen and paper in her hand, doodling those same types of curly-cues. She'd gifted Aubrey with one of her pages of doodles. Tesla would have been proud of the freehand designs. And she treasured the gift, which lay framed and safely tucked in her suitcase.

If she turned around and went home, she'd have to listen to Mara's consternation for days or weeks on end. Maybe she should spend a night, check it out. Then, Mara would get off her case and she could get back to the rightful depression she'd been mired in.

The sun was well on its way down the westward path to setting, so she might not make it back to Butte by nightfall. Driving solo on a pitch-black, lonely road wasn't a smart choice. So be it. Aubrey straightened. One night. Anything could be tolerated for one night, right? She started the engine and, since she only had a short way to go, she put the windows up and turned on the blessed air conditioning.

As she headed down the winding driveway, she followed fencing that separated pastures into a perfect, idyllic setting, just like in the movies. This ranch used blond wood fencing that seemed to melt into the view, not stand out. It looked right. On one side, several horses stood, enjoying the late afternoon heat. One neighed, making Aubrey smile as she remembered riding all those years ago. She'd planned to have her own horses by twenty, but life had taken her in a more urban direction. Living in Seattle had left no room for equestrian hobbies. As she neared the ranch house, Aubrey noticed a lone horse in a fenced area on the other side. Aubrey squinted to get a better view in the sunshine. A brown and white, very dirty horse watched her with troubled, soulful eyes while she drove past.

She parked in front of a two-story, sprawling house. Having never been on a ranch before, Aubrey only had movies to guide her perception. This didn't stray far from those ideals. With a wrap-around porch and siding that looked like reclaimed barn wood, it didn't look old. Rather, it looked homey, with brushes of color in standing and hanging flower pots. Chairs, gliders, and small tables dotted the porch and an American flag hung from a small post jutting out above white-washed stairs that invited you to enter.

Stepping out of the car, Aubrey took a deep breath. At that moment, as she gazed around, peace filled her to the point she didn't want to move. To stay here, to feel a tranquility foreign to her these days, was a blessing. Aubrey closed her eyes and turned her face to the sun, accepting the heat as part of what made this moment feel good.

She couldn't stand there forever, though, so she popped the trunk and pulled out her suitcase, closing it quietly. She didn't want to disturb the serenity. Before she headed inside to locate someone, she looked back at the lone horse. He stood on the far side of the pasture and she could see him shivering. She set her suitcase down, her feet drawn toward the fence, her eyes focused on the horse. Something had hurt him. She could sense the pain, feel the fear.

The horse held her gaze as she reached for the wood fence slat. She stood there, silent and still, waiting. It took a while, but the horse stepped in her direction, moving toward her like one of those slow-motion commercials with Clydesdales. Except this was no workhorse. This boy was sleek and dappled in the white and brown striations of a pinto. Aubrey couldn't remember anything or anyone looking as handsome as this guy, even though the matting and mud-caking of his hair had turned the white patches to a dull gray.

The strangest sensation filled her as the horse got closer, as if she was coming home. When the horse stopped in front of her, Aubrey reached out her hand.

"Stop!"

***

More information about this story and more by Laurie Ryan can be found on her website.